The Quiet Ones

Cheryce Clayton

The Quiet Ones

Published by Six Point Press

Copyright 2016 Cheryce Clayton

Table of Contents

Chapter 1

Projected Earth date: May 2106

UN Colony Transport Ship: Peirs Anon in Orbit of Rex Tyrol, Designated Choctaw Emigration planet, Kanto Corporation

Fifty-three-year-old Lieutenant Colonel John Phillips stood at the front of the bay and waited for his new men to climb free of their transport pods. Waking up to find themselves physically hot-linked was an unwelcome shock, and he watched them realize there was a cryo-sleep they weren't warned about. He let them broadcast serious irritation into the link and through the group, adding his own sub-vocal growl to the mix to cue his officers and NCOs to the severity of their mission.

It didn't take two minutes before the awareness of the absence of any female Marines rippled through the group of two hundred men. Phillips pulled his mind outside of the link and refused to acknowledge the silent half-questions that pushed against him as the lack of women was confirmed through the link. A female

Pro-gen Marine was the equal to a male Pro-gen and the unstated Policy of the US Marine Corps was that any off-world mission was fifty percent female to fifty percent male to give a shot at colonizing should they become stranded. The two hundred male Pro-gen Marines wearing Colonial pips in front of him represented over one-third of all current Pro-gen males in the Fleet.

Training and emotional feedback quieted the room as the Marines started working their way through the wake-up stretches necessary after a long cryo-sleep. Projected thoughts of going for coffee in the ship's mess competed with half-formed curses in the telepathic background noise. The mission brief specified four-point-seven years in stasis, but Phillips' repaired shoulder told him it had been a lot longer.

Westover, Phillips thought in a tight beam.

Sir! the Navy Corpsman threw back, and Phillips saw the man stand to attention on the other side of the large open bay of the UN ship.

Estimated length of cryo? Phillips asked. He felt the medic's mind slide into his own body on the hot-link, felt the other man concentrate on his heart and then his shoulder. Easing the nerve pinch in his neck by deliberately relaxing his body's posture a bit and pulling a deeper breath into his lungs, Phillips worked to blank his thoughts and concerns about the mission as the medic finished his physical assessment and moved out of Phillips' body and back into his own.

Easy ten years, sir, Westover sent back.

My orders say four-point-seven years, Phillips stated, without glancing back down at his screen.

I'm sure they do, sir. Under five makes the paperwork legal, Westover replied with a bitter emotional flavor to the projected telepathic thought.

Dismissed, Phillips replied and focused to break the link for a moment. He watched the medic relax across the room. Outside of the hot-link, Phillips allowed himself a moment of anger at being lied to and sent on a mission in one long jump that jeopardized his and his men's long-term health. A ten-year cryo was long enough to damage cellular integrity and, even though he and his men were genetically perfect thanks to Pro-gen therapy, Phillips had already spent an accumulated thirty years in cryo. That, combined with the inevitable exotic radiations and toxic chemical exposures, meant that he hadn't felt perfect in a very long time.

The hot-link pushed against his brain with the sensation of a full-blown migraine and Phillips took a second to breathe deeply and drain his emotions back into his core and out of broadcast range. The hot-link was designed for short missions; it was impossible to ignore for more than a minute or two, and difficult to think through with the noise of the other men's active thoughts a dull roar inside his head. The Pro-gen telepathy he could block, the physical thoughts from the firing of electricity inside the other brains, he couldn't.

It sounded like his own half-formed thoughts, like ideas floating just under his awareness that if he quit blocking them, would fully form and be his. Times two hundred, most with only basic levels of training.

Phillips closed his eyes, listened for anyone in trouble or overwhelmed, and in the absence of frightened or angry thought-voices, smiled tightly and moved two steps to the left to catch the attention of his Marines.

"Eyes forward. We are on a bug hunt; the planet has a recurring hatching of nasties and we are going to drop, rock, and roll. The planet is a piece of work and the colonists are not aware of our assistance. Command gives us a fifty-fifty chance and the Blue-hatted Captain has authorization to drop a nuke if we fail."

Having drawn their complete attention, Phillips waited for several frozen men to process what he said and then finish putting their drop-suits on. The suits were considered OSFA – One-Size-Fits-Andy – and pulling the stretchable forms over tight muscles and getting the ports in the right places without pinching took concentration.

The last few men tested helmet locks and O2 reserves before giving a thumbs up. Phillips took two steps to the right, turned, and scanned the room before starting.

"We are going to eradicate the bugs in short order because we also have orders…," Phillips paused for effect and threw a quick, tight-beamed thought of concern to his command staff. "…to impregnate as many local women as possible before extraction."

A few mental bursts of excitement were quickly tamped down as sergeants turned to look questioningly at those whose minds went first to rape.

"We burn out the bugs by any means necessary. We seduce the women of legal fucking age and leave a gallon of sperm behind for later use. Am I clear?" Phillips didn't give them time to respond. He triggered the intel video and resumed talking.

"Our objective is dead center, gentlemen. The corporate emigration colony of Rex Tyrol; locals call it 'Coyote's Winter House'. It is a cold rock. Three rivers with no rhyme or reason to their flow. Covered by hostile flora in the form of giant trees that pin prey to their trunks like colossal Venus flytraps. Stay away from the trees." The blue-gray trees in the projected video looked delicate and feathery until a settler's cow walked up, and the camera zoomed in to show it step on an exposed root. The camera zoomed back out as the tree snapped three rows of branches and leaves down. The cow disappeared into a lump on the side of the tree, and the video panned out further to show a wall of trees, each trunk more than twenty feet across.

"The colonists use rocks to make pathways. We will need to stay on paths, in cultivated fields, and on riverbanks. The native ground cover is a saw grass, emphasis on the saw." The video showed a man running the flat head of a shovel across a patch of long-bladed grass. Scratches in the metal glinted as the man swung the dew-wet shovel back and forth. "Think titanium razor and cyanide lube. Our suits will allow limited contact; don't try taking a stroll. You will not survive the grass."

"The settlement has a branch of one of the main rivers to the compass North by Northeast and two small rivers that feed to and from a second main river to the South and Southeast. The rivers have large mollusks on their banks; they eat people. Keep your eyes open; they are easy to spot. The waters hold at least forty-seven differently classed squid-like creatures, the bigger the body of water the bigger the squid – yeah, they are going to try to eat you, too."

The Ship's Captain entered the room and the briefing stopped.

Two hundred US Marines on Colonial orders shifted as one to stare straight ahead and not acknowledge the UN Merchant Marine Captain.

"Can I help you, sir?" Phillips asked bluntly.

"No, carry on," the Captain said and held his place just inside the bay doors.

"This mission is Colonial Marines, Sir. Briefing is confidential," Colonel Phillips said without breaking eye contact with the other officer. The cryo migraine throbbed through the hot-link as he waited for the other man.

"As you were," the Ship Captain said, pivoting to leave, as if his order had any sway over the Marines waiting for their drop to rescue the Colony.

As you weren't, Phillips broadcast, and the men in the room chuckled.

The collective laugh caught the Ship Captain as the bay airlock closed and Phillips saw his frown through the window before it fogged. His fear of Pro-gen, telepaths, and Marines broadcast through the men, and Phillips watched them smirk with pride.

The United States Marine Corps was the elite, and to be accepted into the Colonial Marine Expeditionary Force was a level of elite few could ever hope for. To have survived the scientists and received a telepathy rating advanced enough to earn a hot-link was the top of the elite. On Earth, Phillips had been given his pick of available Pro-gen Colonial Marines for the mission and of the six hundred and eighty-two men who qualified, two hundred were sitting in front of him now. He didn't know why the UN or the Japanese Corporate placed such a high value on the rock, but he and his men would secure it. And the fact that their mission included changing the genetic make-up of the future generations of settlers was just a bonus.

"As I was saying, gentlemen. The planet is a bitch. They've lost the colony twice before to the infestations."

The video showed an insect the size of a man's hand crawling on the back of a cow. It was metallic blue, shot through with teal and black streaks. It had a round body like a ladybug, and a tiny face that looked like a clown in pastel green and pink. It opened its wings and shook them out briefly before shifting its weight onto its front set of legs and unfurling a long stinger or probe from under its wings. The stinger was three times as long as the bug and, as it rested on the cow's back, the stinger hardened to look like a sharp, black knife blade. The bug shook its wings once more and this time its painted outer shell fell off, revealing a lean, black insect. Its previously tiny-looking legs stretched out and it stood, turning its nightmare of a face directly toward the camera before leveraging its body to force the knife-edged stinger into the cow's back, directly over the spinal column.

The cow bellowed once before dropping to its knees in an apparent seizure.

The bug pulled the stinger out slowly.

"That, gentlemen, is an ovipositor. It's laid eggs."

And the insect flew toward the camera in a blur. The screen went black and then the video restarted at the point the insect turned toward the camera. The video slowed down and zoomed in, and the men watched the bug pull its ovipositor out with eggs dripping and then lift its wings to fly. The video's speed slowed again and a bright "32X" appeared beside the bug as it flew straight and low past the camera.

"You cannot outrun them. I doubt you can shoot them on the wing. Anyone or thing that has eggs implanted is an immediate threat."

And the video resumed from the point the insect buzzed past. The camera fell to the ground, the system re-oriented its view and the cow could be seen through blue grass. The cow's back swelled, deformed, and while the cow bellowed and gasped for air, its back eroded from within to reveal a dozen large grub worms that then devoured the cow.

Two minutes passed and the Marines watched silently as the pale green worms moved from the body to finish the cow's head. Something dropped in front of the camera and it auto-focused on a man's hand, clenched tight in a fist, wedding ring visible. The camera focused again and revealed the grub that was holding the hand, the wrist bone completely in its hinged jaw, chewing.

"They burn," Phillips said to the quiet room. "Blood alcohol level is high enough that you could probably run them through a still without too much waste. Any questions?"

"How fast are the grubs?" Sergeant Major Bill Metzger asked; others nodded their heads.

"How many grubs hatch per person?" Lance Corporal Lonco asked.

"When do we get laid?" Lance Corporal Trey threw in, and everyone chuckled.

"First we rescue the colony from the bugs, then we get their women pregnant, then we get out of town." Phillips said in a sing-song that brought a smile to the room.

Why is the UN willing to give an Emigration Colony telepathy? Gunnery Sergeant Weistler asked silently, and everyone waited for the response.

"They aren't," Phillips replied. "Seems the planet has a disease that kills men around forty years old and women at menopause. UN gave us a Pro-gen boost while we were under and we, gentlemen, are bringing a genetic resistance to the next generation."

"And no one told the colonists that? Why not give it to new colonists as they ship in?" Trey asked, all serious now.

"Someone decided it was easier to put us through a little extra on the progressive genetic therapy than to talk a bunch of sell-out immigrants into allowing themselves to be altered. Besides, most immigrants would just pick a different planet and they'd have to give up on this one." Phillips didn't bother to add that immigrants never read their contracts and wouldn't understand that the genetic manipulation of the populace was legal, normal, and common. This was his second such mission and the idea of leaving behind a fresh batch of Phillips' DNA was the reason he accepted it.

'Cause it's such a great location for the next Tokyo Towers, Weistler said and projected his bitter paranoia with the thought.

"Can it," Sergeant Major Metzger said without addressing the comment directly.

"The grubs hatch at six to seven inches, grow to eighteen inches, and then burrow underground like cicadas. They have been observed outrunning a man," Phillips said, and the video resumed.

An older man with black hair shot through with gray was running toward the camera. The lens focused in on a green and red grub the size of a large cat that humped behind the man, gaining quickly. The man's terrified face stared at the camera as he struggled to gain speed. The grub got within a few feet of the running man and then spat out a blob of dark blue mucus at the man's left leg. The man fell and the grub was on him, eating between his legs as the man writhed and screamed.

The Marines watching made a show of wincing in sympathy amidst uncomfortable laughter.

"There is no confirmation that the spit is toxic. There is no proof that it is harmless. Do not get close enough to find out for us. The hatch rate seems to correspond with the body mass of the host," Phillips added as the video showed several more cows going down and then one woman.

Do they have a hive mind? Lance Corporal Trey thought over Phillips and several men turned to glance at him as they waited for the answer.

Phillips noted Treys' flash of apology with a slow nod.

"There was no indication of coordinated attacks by the flying bug form, though one radio report stated that the bugs seemed to know which buildings contained survivors and which were empty. The grubs were reported to work as hunting teams from their hatching."

The bastards never dropped. They watched from orbit and collected intel, Weistler interjected, and Phillips frowned at the Gunny.

"The ship reported that the infestation was well established and the few survivors radioed telling them not to land," Phillips said and took a moment to collect himself as the video switched to an orbital view.

"This is Coyote's Winter House, Rex Tyrol, broadcasting a warning to any ship inbound. Bugs came out of the forest and we are dying. I have included the Station password, people put up video and pictures. Don't land. Blow 'em back to hell," a rough male voice said while the planet spun on the screen.

"Note the places without trees; the theory is those are where the bugs are," Phillips said and waited as several large clearings spun past. "That was the first settlement," Phillips said as a sharp-edged crater came into view.

"Sweet," Lonco exclaimed as the size of the crater became apparent.

"Someone overloaded and detonated the grounded colony ship's power station," Phillips acknowledged.

The circle of the nuclear blast crater overlapped the current colony clearing to the Northwest, and as the globe spun, a second blast crater was seen to the South. This one was much smaller and deeper and looked to be filled with water from one of the meandering streams.

"And someone else knew a bit about demolitions. Makes me think the bugs or grubs like the power station. We will be shutting it down cold from orbit before we drop," Phillips concluded, and the wall screen went gray.

"Pack extra batteries; low angle on the star means a limited recharge window with long fucking nights. Dropping in two hours, gentlemen, check your gear, check your armor, and check your partner. Maps are uploading now." And he hit a few more buttons on his control panel. "Leave the Aughts behind and max out on incendiaries. They burn."

"Westover, you're with me," Phillips said, and the young Corpsman stood up and separated from his team.

"Sir?" Westover asked in a neutral voice.

Your opinion on the Gunny? Phillips asked silently and pushed through the other man's shields to see his concern mirrored.

Weistler's a suicide, sir, Westover pushed back, and Phillips watched him work to calm his own anger at the mental invasion of privacy. *Survivor's guilt. He's looking to be a hero.*

"I can work with that," was all Phillips replied verbally.

"Sir," Westover prompted, out loud, after two minutes passed.

Phillips paused in his conversation with his officers. "Dismissed," was the offhand reply as he returned to coordinating the drop sequence, his gaze locked across the room to stare at the back wall that held the now dark video screen.

Chapter 2

Projected Earth date: May 2106

Planet Date: 0079, Fall

Rex Tyrol, Designated Choctaw Emigration planet, Kanto Corporation

Colonel Phillips was not the first on the ground, but only because he landed on some colonist's roof. He rolled and lay on his back, watching his men drop. They were a deep green in his display, while the bugs were bright streaks of yellow that seemed to go for the heat of the static chutes.

Phillips gave half a prayer of thanks that the large chutes' heat signatures were greater than the Marines dropping underneath, as only two men screamed out in pain and then went silent.

The power station was a faint glow to the West, having been shut down via the master code. The UN Ship Captain wished them well and then turned to order the nukes prepped, while Phillips and his men waited to jump and make the long fall through the atmosphere.

The plain fact was that the Corporation sponsoring this colony wanted the bugs gone, and if nuking every clearing from orbit would eradicate them, then the UN would accept the loss of a few thousand immigrants. Putting two hundred expensive Pro-gen Marines on the ground was supposed to act as an inhibiting factor, but Phillips had no doubt that the Ship Captain had already pencil-whipped his paperwork to justify dropping the bombs.

They had three days from planet dawn to understand the enemy and offer a concrete plan for the colonies' continued growth or the planet would be depopulated, deforested, and then turned into a mining factory that shipped in breathing air for its workers. Frontier and farm colonies were just a way to hold a planet while getting tax and political credit until the owner was ready to exploit or develop the rock.

Phillips heard a bug land on the metal roof beside his foot and shifted quickly to fire a short blast from his incendiary rifle. The bug lit up and burned as it slid down the roof, and Phillips watched in horror, scrambling back up the roof and over the ridgeline, as a swarm of six or seven bugs dive-bombed the hot spot he'd created with his weapon.

The incendiary rifle fired a super-heated stream of mercury vapor mixed with ambient air that melted or burned straight through organics and heated most metals to the melting point on contact. It was a short-range saturation weapon that left an environmental mess to clean up afterward. And right now it left a hot-spot that drew the flying bugs right to him.

Don't fire the incendiary rifles! He blasted the thought through the hot-link to every man landing. *The incendiary rifles draw the bugs!*

Fuck! Nearly every Marine thought at once, and Phillips left his own rifle on the roof as he dropped to the ground and started running toward the rendezvous spot.

Switch out for press guns! Greer called.

Burn your chute on landing, then drop your incendiary rifle and run, Metzger offered in a calm focus, and Phillips rebroadcast the order.

A moon flashed bright in the sky and Phillips ripped his night vision up, blinking as he ran.

Someone screamed in his mind, and he silently counted three dead. He didn't bother calling for a head count, the hot-link made him aware of his men as a whole, a few hotheads and one panic attack rode the link and the rest were background to his own thoughts.

The sight of a cow down and three grubs flooded his vision. He watched as someone fired a press gun. The sound waves turned the grubs to water balloons and startled every bug for nearly a mile. Phillips watched from several men's eyes as a swarm of thousands of bugs rose up around them and then circled. The press guns fired up into the swarm several times and half of the bugs fell dead before the mass flew East toward the river.

That was too fucking easy.

Watch yourself, air threat, heading toward the river.

Press guns work.

And for the first time since landing, Phillips had a plan for surviving.

#

"Why didn't they send the Army?" a voice shouted from the middle of the crowd before Phillips could introduce himself.

Noon local and seven hours since the drop, Phillips and three other men stood beside a tall red pole that was worn pink in a band from three feet off the ground to above his head by names and hearts carved into the alien wood as he tried to calm the crowd in front of them.

"God wasn't available, the UN sent my men instead," Phillips said.

No one laughed.

"I am Lieutenant Colonel John Phillips, United States Marine Corps, Battalion 42, Colonial Marines.

We are all Pro-gen Marines and we are here to kill bugs," he said in a forced brag and smiled when people recoiled.

Civilians were always afraid of genetically enhanced Marines and Phillips was of the opinion that they should be. He and his men were hot-linked telepaths, and they were Marines. The progressive genetic therapy gave better health and healing, significant improvements in reflexes, speed, and strength, and sometimes telepathy. The hot-link was an actual implant designed from the old cochlear hearing implants and it tapped into both sight and sound. He could see what others were seeing, they could see what he was seeing, and the Pro-gen telepathy meant they could work as an integrated team. Civilians never understood the Corps and Phillips saw no reason to explain.

"I found a soldier's gun. How many men did you lose?" a woman asked.

"Ma'am, that weapon was dropped for a reason. The incendiary rifles draw the bugs to the weapon's heat signature," Phillips said and saw several people in the crowd shift uncomfortably. "I'm going to repeat this – if you found one of our dropped rifles – the incendiary rifles draw the bugs to you. Save them for after the threat is past, but do not fire them until the bugs are eradicated."

"Turn them in to the Armory and Sheriff Toms will give you an extra ration of ammo for your cartridge arms, no paperwork," the Chief said from beside Phillips.

Chief Gary Lightfeather was young, maybe thirty years old, but colony life had been hard on him. Phillips noted the wet, seeping infection that dampened his shirt at the shoulder and covered his left hand. The man used a cane and wheezed standing still.

Doc. How are we for antibiotics?

Needs antifungals. I got enough for us.

A bunch of them have it.

Shit's creepy.

We at risk?

Don't kiss anyone infected.

Fuck 'em from behind, gotcha.

Silence, Metzger pushed over the telepathic laughter that bled into the hot-link and threatened to become hysterical.

"Thank you," Phillips said with a nod to the local leader.

"We have electric press guns that have been proven to be effective against the bugs. Knocks them right out of the sky," Phillips told the crowd.

"I want one!" someone shouted and people nodded, looking at him expectantly.

"What about the grubs?" another shouted.

"The press guns were effective against the grubs. No, you can't have mine," and he tried to make it a joke but the colonists just stared back at him with frightened eyes. "We are short on juice and would ask anyone with charged Class 7 or newer power packs to make them available ASAP."

"Do you know why that weapon worked?" the Chief asked from beside him when no one in the crowd stepped forward to offer battery packs.

"An electric press gun fires a ball of sound. The bugs are drawn to heat, seem to see in infrared. The grubs are drawn to movement, one Marine remained still and a pack of grubs went past him to attack a cow. I would theorize that the bugs are vulnerable to any concussive blast or wave. Tonight we will draw them out and wipe them out." Phillips decided that the town hall was over and turned and walked from the red pole to the edge of the clearing were several of his men were waiting.

Colonel? the Doc said clearly and Phillips tightened the link.

Yeah?

Where are the old people?

This batch of colonists started landing twenty-six years ago. UN's landing more people every five years. No time to get old.

Feels wrong. Should be a few gray hairs landing in each batch.

What are you thinking?

That infection. Kids don't have it.

Does it affect our current mission?

No, sir. It's the why of our secondary mission.

Then don't worry about it now, Doc.

And Phillips released the link and felt the others seep into his brain. Travers was injured, Weistler angry, Trey was fucking some woman in a barn while Lonco stood watch, and Petley was jacking off to Trey's conquest while two kids watched him from behind a tree. Everyone else was a blur of similar thoughts and scenery.

"Sheriff Toms will give you the tour," the chief said, and Phillips knew he had been talking for a minute, had trusted Metzger to cue him if anything important was said while he checked on his men telepathically.

"Thank you," Phillips said and refocused on the sheriff.

Kid doesn't need to shave, someone chimed over the link, and Phillips worked to keep the frown off of his own face.

25

"My dad died two nights ago. I know the security codes and no one wants to step up," the kid explained quietly without being asked.

Fuck.

"You're doing fine," Phillips said. "Show us around and we'll see what we can do about saving a few lives."

"Yes sir," the teen replied and almost smiled.

\#

"When do you think we can put the power station back online?" Acting Sheriff JJ Toms asked as they finally reached the West lookout tower.

The tour had taken them along the river, through two planted fields and a gap in one of the eroded rock ridges. The smaller ridges' heights varied from five- to ten-feet tall as they spiraled out from the center of the valley. Toms led them beyond the plastic greenhouses to a path through an open field of native saw grass that led to the second colony's arc of abandoned houses and the blast crater lake.

The whole time the kid apologized for not having an electric cart to drive and pointed out character flaws in the people they met. The five-story wooden lookout tower sat on top of an intersection of the smaller ridgelines. The rock radiated out from the center of the valley and met the near forty-foot high Western ridge that framed the valley. The lookout towers were built on the ridges and the kid explained that they were used in the spring when a native predator came out of the surrounding forest to hunt and mate.

"Last two times the bugs swarmed, the power stations blew up," Phillips said and pointed across the colony valley to the obvious crater. "I ordered your station offline until the hatch is over," and he saw no need to mention the trigger-happy UN Ship Captain in orbit with a dozen nukes at the ready.

"Oh," the kid said, and Phillips realized that no one had told the colonists.

"This is the third hatching; we have the bugs figured out." Phillips pointed to the lake, realized that the kid had never seen it as a crater, and turned his back on the valley to watch the boy in his peripheral vision.

"What do you know about the bugs?" Phillips asked.

"A few showed up at the barns last week. Killed Jeff Vernehey and seven cows overnight." The kid stared out at the valley behind Phillips. "My dad and Joey Sinclare killed a bunch of flying bugs with shotguns before grubs attacked and killed Joey. Dad said the shotguns killed the grubs, but there were hundreds of bugs in the air and grubs on the ground and he hid in the meat smoker until morning. Almost coughed himself to death."

"The smoker was hot?" Phillips asked softly, staring out across a field of saw grass at the blue-gray wall of trees.

"Yeah, winter's coming. We slaughtered the extra pigs last week. They're in the smoke."

The bugs don't like smoke, Phillips thought.

Start arranging for smudge fires, Metzger ordered.

"My dad was going to go out and hunt some more the next night, but him and some guys decided to check on the barns first. Must have been a thousand grubs. They just burned the barns and watched the fires all night. The bugs stayed away from the barns burning. Guess they attacked people over by second camp instead…" the kid trailed off, staring out without seeing, and Phillips glanced over and thought about putting a hand on his shoulder. But the pain coming from the kid was obvious without telepathy.

"And then?" Phillips prompted.

"It rained for three days, that's why the rivers are high," the kid said, and Phillips took a second look at the muddy river in the distance.

Easily two miles across, the main river was brown and greasy looking as it flowed toward a break in the West ridge line. To the South, he looked past the crater lake to see the smaller river that moved in the opposite direction and tumbled down the ridge in a waterfall that was a dull hiss in the distance. There was a high ridgeline past the Southern river and he knew from his orbital maps that another river was hidden on its far side, just before the looming trees.

"Why didn't they warn us?" the kid demanded, and the anger seemed to push away his pain, for a moment. "They sent you, so they knew. They could have warned us."

"They thought we would get here a month ahead of time so we could get you ready," Phillips lied, and Weistler's anger screamed through his mind.

Doc! Phillips shouted mentally and felt the medic concentrate on Weistler until the other faded into the background.

"The bugs didn't come out in the rain?" Phillips asked the kid.

"No. The grubs drowned, the bugs walked around but couldn't fly, and we hunted them in the rain with torches and shotguns. We thought we got all of them," the kid was whispering and Phillips knew something bad had happened.

"You didn't," he prompted.

"No." And the kid stared out over the colony. "No, sir."

"I need to know what happened," Phillips prodded.

"Two nights ago some houses slid into the river. My dad and some guys went to help get people clear of the nearby houses," the kid drew a breath. "The rain stopped just before first dawn."

Phillips paused at the mention of first dawn.

"First dawn?" he asked to give the kid an excuse to draw out of the memory. A buffer of facts against the pain.

"We have three moons," the kid said and Phillips nodded. "There's a fat brown one that sits in the sky from sunset until an hour before dawn. The sun hits it and it's a golden mirror. No warning," the kid explained and Phillips remembered getting blinded with his night vision and losing three men for lack of warning.

"What happened before first dawn, when it stopped raining?" Phillips asked.

"Someone on the radio said the ground was boiling bugs," the kid answered and turned his back on the colony. "I don't know. No one outside survived. They were just gone."

The kid wasn't crying and Phillips didn't offer a hand on his shoulder for comfort. Instead he offered respect and hoped the kid understood.

"Thank you, Sheriff," Phillips said.

#

"Careful," a woman said as Westover left Weistler and made his way back toward the town center. Something swooshed behind him and he jumped clear without looking as Lonco took over his body like a puppet to get him clear of the threat.

"Fuck!" he said and let his irritation at the hot-link flood him for a moment. That the other man had been able to take control so easily told him Lonco had more than an average telepathy rating.

You're welcome, echoed through his mind with a chuckle from the Marine standing in front of him.

"The hunter almost got you," the woman said and Westover looked over to see her standing in her doorway watching him.

"Why didn't it go for the guy in front of me?" Westover asked. There had been a local walking on the path, closer to the tree, and he had passed unharrassed.

"The young trees in town are domesticated. They like us, we talk to them. They don't know you," she said, and Lonco pushed in his mind to point out her nipples under the thin blouse and the fact that she was obviously curious about him.

Secondary mission, Westover thought without patience and didn't try to hide the fact that he did not find the short, weather-worn woman attractive.

Faggot, someone thought back at him, mostly as a joke, and Westover pushed back an image of a Marine giving a blow job to another in the shower before the drop.

Dead meat, a new thought hit hard, not joking.

Children! Metzger shot through the link and Westover felt his annoyance.

Sorry, Mom, Lonco threw back, and several minds chuckled before focusing on their surroundings and not Westover.

"Well, then, ma'am, I guess we need to get better acquainted with these trees," Lonco said, and Westover nodded to the woman and then moved to continue down the trail. "Could I trouble you to introduce me to a few trees? It might help," and the blond Marine got the woman to blush.

Anyone get a telepathic read on the trees? Lonco asked and Westover felt several men shift their minds.

It was old, hungry, and bored; when the first Marine telepath touched its mind, it pounced and tried to ride the link back into his body with a force that brought every Marine to a frozen stop.

God damn Christ almighty! What the fuck is that? Phillips demanded and Westover broke himself clear of the hot-link for a moment to think. But the link reformed and everyone was shouting and the old mind was in the link too loud to ignore and overwhelmingly alien.

Westover focused everything he had on Phillips. Felt his heartbeat, tasted his air, and then pulled Trey into the heartbeat. Lonco followed. Metzger grabbed Weistler mentally and the two of them pushed through to hold a few more minds separate from the invader. Within a minute the old mind was pushed out and the Marines each took a separate breath, and looked around to assess their situations.

Okay. Don't talk to the trees. They might answer.

And a tree seemed to chuckle near Westover.

#

Trey was in a house, consoling another widow, when Phillips scanned his men. *That won't get her pregnant,* Lonco quipped and Phillips grinned along with the rest of his team as they moved through the rain, looking for bugs.

Stick to the secondary mission, cowboy, the ever serious Metzger added as Trey shifted positions with the woman and the intensity of his pleasure flooded the link.

Oh, a voice exclaimed and Phillips felt several of the less experienced Marines get seriously distracted from their surroundings.

Finish up, Phillips threw across the line. *Check your partner,* he added with a physical glance over to see Westover walking beside him. A lone bug sat on a fence rail beside the medic, unable to fly in the rain. Phillips nodded toward the bug and Lonco tapped it with a baseball bat.

The cold rain started just before sunset and showed no sign of abating. A radio-check with the ship in orbit confirmed a large expanse of wet clouds moving in and, from previous observation, the ship monitor had offered a paycheck bet that the rain lasted two days.

The rain kept the bugs down and prevented the Marines from doing their job and that was dangerous bad news as the clock ticked toward the nuclear deadline.

The sheriff kid is coming, Metzger called over the link.

Phillips switched off his night vision, trusting Lonco to spot for him, and pushed the goggles up out of his way. The night was black and shiny, and reflected light from torches and lanterns gave the illusion of enough light to see by on the path.

The sheriff carried a bright flashlight that he swung back and forth, lighting the edges of the path from left to right and back to left as he approached the waiting Marines. Phillips could feel the kid's fear and telepathically picked up the whisper of the internal conversation the kid was having to keep himself moving and not paralyzed with terror.

"Problem, Sheriff?" Phillips asked in a soft voice when he realized that the kid had focused his vision on the bright spot that the flash made and lost his night vision. The Marines carried low light, green-lensed hand-lights, but relied on their night vision to show them the infrared, the heat signatures, and to magnify available light. The kid had a single LED focused-beam flashlight and an old pump action shotgun. Phillips didn't begrudge him his fear in the night.

"Megan LittleFeather radioed that her house was cracking and then never responded to repeated calls. I'm walking over to check on her," the kid explained, blinking the rain out of his eyes as he tried to spot Phillips in the dark.

"Close your eyes," Phillips said, and nodded to himself when the kid obeyed. "Now, when you open your eyes, look to the darkest spot you can see and stare for a solid minute. Keep the flashlight down," he added.

And the kid did as he was told. Phillips watched him through Lonco's night vision and saw his pupils adjust to the night.

"Better?" Phillips asked, and the kid turned and looked straight at him, making eye contact.

"Yeah, thanks."

"You can move the flashlight around, just don't stare at the light. You'll see a bug if the light hits it; they shine like metal in this rain," Phillips said and turned to walk beside the kid. "How far to Miss LittleFeather's house?"

"It's on the edge of the new raspberry fields, almost to the river."

"By the last sinkhole?" Phillips asked as they walked, Westover following, Lonco walking ahead.

"Not quite. Her house is at the edge of the arc before the forest drops in. The other sinkhole was where the forest meets the river."

River must be undercutting the bank, Metzger said and silently directed fourteen men to move away from the river edge.

Twelve responded.

Petley, Travers, report, Phillips forced loudly but there was silence where there should have been two minds.

Anyone hear anything? Metzger asked, still scanning for the dead men.

Negative.

No copy.

Negative.

And Phillips blocked his own thought that Trey's orgasm must have drowned out the loss of the men. Westover broadcast a similar half-formed thought and Phillips felt Trey recoil from the link.

Let it go, he ordered and realized that the sheriff was talking.

"After this is over?" Phillips heard the kid finish and Lonco mentally shrugged, having missed the conversation as well.

Wants to be a Marine or Pro-gen, wasn't clear, Westover said.

"I think you are a strong candidate and I would be honored to sign a letter of recommendation for you," Phillips said and meant it.

"Thank you, sir," and the kid's relief was picked up and rebroadcast into the link.

And Phillips felt Lonco tamp down and disengage.

What IS your rating? Westover demanded, but Lonco was blocking and Phillips ignored him to focus on the kid.

Lance Corporal Lonco was an S5 active telepath with a heavy empathy rating. Phillips had fought to get him on his team, despite the black ink in his file. Like Metzger, Lonco was easily capable of holding the hot-linked collective of minds if something happened to Phillips. Trey and Weistler were the only other Marines on the planet with a rating high enough to take control of the hot-link and force a command, but neither had the training. Westover was a medic and that meant his hot-link filtered out all emotions, allowed him to step outside if he needed to and not get swept up in the moment. Phillips was impressed by the young Doc and the fact that he had held the link against the tree mind until Mezger stepped in.

"It's just ahead," the kid said and gestured to the left, at a fork in the road.

Negative, Lonco said and Phillips mentally saw the path drop away into the swirl of the angry river.

"Stay here," Phillips ordered and mentally included Westover to stay with the kid in the dark as he pulled his night vision back down and jogged toward Lonco.

The river had washed out the trail. One house sat precariously close to the edge, and Lonco was detecting frightened people inside.

Get 'em out. How many houses nearby? Phillips threw at Westover to ask the kid, then waited impatiently for an answer.

No clue, Westover replied and gave a mental image of the kid pushing past him to continue toward the disaster.

Give him your goggles, Phillips ordered.

Westover and the kid came into sight as Lonco herded a woman and two kids out of the house and back down the path.

"Maria," the kid said in shock. Two Marines stepped into sight, press guns at ready and watched over the civilians after a nod from Phillips.

"You can take them to safety," Westover offered and Phillips frowned at the medic's annoyance of losing his goggles.

"Give the Doc your goggles and escort them back to the town center," Phillips said out loud for the civilians' benefit. "How many more houses in this area?" Phillips prodded the kid, who stared at the new-cut riverbank in shock.

"Two hundred. Two hundred houses between here and the river," and the kid pointed straight out at the rippling water. "They're just gone."

"We lost two men without any sound," Phillips said. Trying to give the kid something to distract him.

"Your telepathy?" the kid turned to ask, and Westovers' goggles shifted on his face to give him a slanted, questioning pose.

"Just gone. They never knew what hit them. Had to be almost instant," Phillips said and pushed the thought across the link for Trey to feel.

"But drowning isn't fast. And Megan said her house was shifting and breaking. She had time to call me."

Phillips nodded as he surveyed the crumbling edge of the riverbank. The empty house shifted in the rain and he gave a mental order for all men to get well clear of the river for the night.

"There's no point to us being out in this rain. Everybody find a dry spot and shut your eyes," Phillips said out loud.

The sheriff gave him a puzzled look, until Squad Three stepped out of the dark from beside the shifting house and nodded, before fading into the dark again.

No fucking around, get some rest, Metzger added. Sleep was impossible with the hotlink.

#

"And this map is current?" Lonco asked.

"Yes, it was," Chief Gary Lightfeather said. The man had aged overnight and Phillips was concerned about being in the same room with the slick black fungus that could be seen on the chief's hand.

"Are you contagious?" Weistler demanded.

Lightfeather turned away from the map spread out on the table in the makeshift emergency command center. The room used to be the colony preschool and no one bother to try sitting in the small chairs that were pushed and piled into the far corner.

"Probably. Everyone gets the rot," and the concern the other man expressed was for them and not himself.

Fuck.

We are immune, gentlemen, that's why we get to fuck like bunnies when the bugs are gone, Westover broadcast. Phillips smiled at the similarity to his own voice as the young medic worked to assert himself against the revulsion Weistler was broadcasting into the link.

"You were saying?" Lonco prompted the chief, and the sick man took a deep breath and refocused on the map of the colony.

"Five miles from North to South and nine miles from East to West. The main river is here, was here," and his voice shook. He was pointing down at a bend in the river and the marked housing block that disappeared in the night. The larger river had come out of the forest and looped into the silver grass clearing for a mile, only now the river entered the clearing from the trees, and over a mile square of occupied land was missing.

Phillips glanced down at the map. "This is where the first colony was; they put their power plant against the trees and built out in a fan. The blast from the power plant took everything but their crops. This is where the second colony put their power station," he pointed to the oval lake that was between the large crater and the South river.

"We were told it was disease. We burned their houses and barns," Lightfeather said.

"You were lied to," Weistler replied, ignoring Phillips' frown.

"Your power station is here, on the river," and Phillips saw the pattern. Saw the intelligence behind the threat.

Lonco, isolate yourself from the link, reach out for the bugs. Westover, monitor him. The trees are awake. I think I'm seeing an intelligent threat from the bugs, Phillips thought and continued to stare down at the map with the new sinkholes and river path drawn in red over the colony.

"You need to evacuate here, here, and here," Phillips said and continued the arc past the power station.

Fuck, Weistler thought.

"Oh, fuck," the chief whispered as Phillips drew a dotted line through the seventeen sinkholes and the riverbank undercut. It was clear that something was working at pulling the power station into the river.

"Move people to the East and South," Phillips said and Lonco fell to the floor beside him.

What happened? Phillips demanded as the Marine's eyes rolled into his head and his body stiffened violently.

Shut up, the medic replied and Phillips could feel his concentration.

"Everybody outside, give the Doc room to work," Weistler said and escorted the colonials out of the room.

Phillips knelt beside Westover and silently offered his mind to boost the Doc's attempt to pull Lonco back into his own body.

It was a tree mind, old and bored, that blasted through the link and forced Lonco back into his body. The seizure that followed hit twenty Marines, and Phillips fought the mental chaos and pain, even as he pulled away from Westover.

You good? he asked Lonco as the other man worked to sit up against Westover's wishes.

Yeah, was the reply.

The bugs? he pushed.

Focused anger and hunger, maybe a hive mind, it was a big empty place I couldn't see out of, Lonco tried to explain, without letting images or impressions into the link. He was shook up and Phillips could sense the edge of fear in his mind.

A tree put you back, Westover said and quit trying to force Lonco to be still.

Trees, Lonco corrected. *They're all linked. I could see them stretching back through time and circling the planet. Something else, too. Couldn't see it but it was there.*

Sentient? Phillips asked.

The trees? Absolutely. They laughed at me, like trying to talk to the bugs was a stupid move, but they let me make the mistake and then pulled me back. Trying to teach us a lesson.

Damn.

Check your partner, Phillips sent through the link as the amount of migraine pain continued to grow.

Westover stood and ran from the room without explanation. Phillips searched the link to find a man unconscious on a path, a gloveless hand flung into the poisonous silver grass.

#

"We did them a favor," Phillips explained to the gathered colonists. "The bugs do not like bright light and are working to destroy the power station, when we powered it down, we helped them."

Several people in the crowd nodded their heads, but the crowd was subdued and waiting overall.

"The ship has sent the signal to reboot, and the power station will be back online shortly. Recharging our press guns is the first priority. Lantern batteries are second."

It was dusk, and still raining, though the ship was reporting breaks in the weather pattern and the wind had picked up. The sinkholes continued to swallow houses in an arc that brought the river to within twenty yards of the power station. The ship was directing two locals in rebooting the power system manually and the area around the station was evacuated with everyone hiding in houses and burning smoky fires.

"We will be stationed to protect the population clusters," Phillips continued. The colony was now less than eight hundred people, mostly kids, and the Marines spent the day going door-to-door and moving people to the only defendable position in the colony. At the center of the clearing was an outcropping of bedrock that radiated to the ridgelines. It was the worn down top of an ancient mountain and the ground around it was boulders and gravel for two hundred feet. That was too uneven for the large prefab barns and instead had twenty small stone houses hand-built in an arc around a giant fire pit and a dozen even smaller stone smokehouses. The children were clustered in the houses while the adults fed the smudge fire in the center and added fuel to the smokers to keep a thick haze going in the rain. The wind was their enemy.

"I want everyone here to understand that this power station is going into that river and may overload and detonate." Phillips gestured behind him without turning to look. Several Marines were monitoring the station reboot from inside with the civilian engineers. Four long cords stretched away from the station and almost cleared the projected sinkhole path.

"The bugs are underneath us right now. They see heat signatures, so we are going to give them some hot spots to focus on," he said and nodded to Weistler and Squad Nine as the Marines hefted incendiary rifles and moved North of the power station and closer to the river.

They fired a thin stream of heat at the ground and aimed at the river edge, moving as if people were walking and surveying the area.

Where Phillips and the surviving colonists were standing to watch, piles of ice had been dumped on the ground around them.

Minutes passed and Phillips checked his men twice before a fresh shot at the ground by Weistler was greeted by a small hole and then the ground was replaced by a seething roil of bugs. The sinkhole was ten feet across and the bugs swarmed out and over each other, searching for the heat source before they sank back into the ground and were gone. The hole they left near the riverbank quickly filled with water.

Weistler shifted his aim further North of the riverbank, away from the power station. The bugs responded immediately with the same violent swarm, leaving another ten-foot hole in their wake.

"They haven't attacked anyone on a path; the crushed rock is a barrier, but I'm not going to trust it much. The fields and people's yards are not safe. Don't group together; it concentrates your heat signature. And don't sit or lay on the ground," Phillips finished.

Lines are hot, Allans broadcast.

Get everyone out of there, Metzger replied.

Yes, Sergeant Major. Allans succeeded in putting a hint of sarcasm into the thought and Phillips felt a few men smile. The kid had fallen, his right hand in the silver grass, and only Westover's quick decision to amputate the hand saved his life. Now he was hopped up on pain meds with his wrist tightly bandaged at the amputation site. Westover was pissed that he wasn't in one of the safe houses with a herd of colonial brats.

"Let's get plugged in and recharged," Phillips said out loud as his men started swapping press gun battery packs for charging.

The electric weapons were good for twenty full-power shots on a battery; each Marine had five issued batteries. Some had reclaimed more from their fallen brothers. Most Marines spent three batteries the first night on the ground. The weapon system came with an advanced photocell charger that strapped to your bicep and charged the battery bank. The constant rain interfered with the charging, and Phillips was down to five shots on his own weapon, while men like Lonco wielded improvised hand-to-hand weapons until they could get recharged.

It took seven minutes to charge a pack of four to fifty percent, another ten minutes for a full charge. Phillips watched as men swapped out at the fifty percent mark, working to get as many functional weapons as possible.

Allans and the civilians from the power station exited the grounded shuttle as the last of the dusk sun faded into the rain and wind. Phillips watched them moving along the path toward the group waiting to charge lanterns. The ice piles had melted in the rain and Phillips decided to send most of the civilians on to the safe houses without the lanterns.

Ground shifted, someone said, and every Marine focused, looking for the source and evaluating their own position.

Phillips watched Allans shout and start the civilians running. The young Marine waited until everyone with him was moving faster before he moved to follow, and then slowed to help an older man who couldn't keep up.

The power cords shifted on the ground and someone swore as he lunged to grab a charger before the cord whipped away in the dark.

Allans bent double and then straighten up with the slower man in an awkward, one-handed fireman's carry, his weapon nearly tangling his legs from its sling as he ran.

"Clear!" Phillips shouted out loud, and felt it echo through the line, as the power station slid into the river. Thirty feet of bank were just gone.

Clear! several Marines responded.

Allans slowed to a walk as he approached the civilians, turning to stare at the missing power station.

#

The cluster of small houses was a welcome sight in the light drizzle. The night wasn't dark; a small, yellow moon flashed in and out of the shifting clouds as the wind picked up and the rain faded.

Phillips smelled fuel alcohol and smoked ham before the wind shifted and a thin curtain of smoke slid past them on the path. Sage, moldy plant matter, cooking pork, and something rum-like hit him and his stomach tried to growl. Since landfall he could only remember consuming one ration bar and two canteens of water.

Hydrate, he ordered out of habit, and Westover handed him one of the local's clay jars, full of water, before he could focus on his men.

Everyone inside the smoke, Metzger added with a forced image of the cluster of houses and the fire ring.

Roger that, Lonco added, and Phillips saw himself from the other man's eyes. Every rooftop had four or five Marines, some laying on their backs watching up and around, others face down and staring down over the roof edges and out, all with night vision on waiting for the rain to stop and the bugs to fly.

Someone handed Phillips a piece of fried bread, split open, with shredded meat and a sweet sauce. He let his press gun hang from his sling in front of him as he accepted the food without forfeiting his refilled water.

Weistler threw an image at him of a dim heat signature following beside the path he had just taken, some fifty feet out from the start of the rock outcropping. Phillips boosted the image across the link with a question, and the Marines on the roofs looked out and down. The ground moved in green so bright it looked more white, and it was obvious that the bugs were underground in an arc, two hundred and twenty degrees round, waiting. The heat signature was strongest to the North, between the cluster of houses and the river, and men adjusted their positions as Phillips pushed his final bite into his mouth, untasted, and drank his water.

Last call on the latrine, Trey joked. But the rain stopped, the wind was easing, and Phillips saw the hot clusters grow into a solid circle nearly surrounding the little enclave.

"Light the fields, fuel the smudge fires, it's time," Phillips said to the civilians near him.

The sheriff was on the far side of the fire talking to a group of about twenty young men who had painted their faces and stood holding ornate wooden clubs, waiting for the enemy, ready to defend those working the fires. A single large drum was covered with an umbrella and the chief kept time with Phillip's heartbeat.

A trail of fuel was lit, and Phillips watched the flame snake from the safety of the smudge fires that circled the houses and out into the fields that surrounded them. The corn to the South caught first and as it blazed up, so did the bugs in that field.

In the eyes of the Marines with night vision, the field was a mix; the white of the waiting bugs and the dull orange where the fuel had been poured on the plants hours before. There was a sudden burst of green from the flashover of flames as the fire took on a bloom of almost white that launched into the sky, circled once and flew with the wind in a bright cloud toward the barns. It left the field with an echo of the violent light with enough bright spots left to worry those scanning for danger.

The wheat field to the Southeast took next, and the bugs could be seen without night vision as the clouds parted and the yellow moon lit the night bright enough to read by. The bugs rose up, a black cloud of clicking and a deep hum that filled the sky. It made Phillips aware of his own breathing as the cloud circled the field once, flew through a cloud of smoke, and turned to head toward the South river.

The moon hampered the night vision and Phillips ordered most of the men to flip up their goggles, leaving a handful to struggle though and monitor the darker areas of the surrounding ground and cloudy patches.

The raspberry field never really lit; snakes of flame danced in the field where the fuel pooled, but the plants were too green and wet to burn. The smoldering field never bloomed with bugs and Weistler used his incendiary rifle to hit a few hot patches a hundred yards out from the roof he was on. The bugs roiled up and were gone with each shot as Weistler adjusted his aim.

Quit fuckin' around, Metzger said as Weistler drew a slow arc in the field to complete his masterpiece. A penis drawn in fire and sinkholes.

Trey pushed into the link with an image of thousands of bugs roiling up and circling to the West in a solid black cloud.

Coming back, Lonco said with a sharp image of a cloud of bugs moving fast from the river.

Shit, Metzger added, as the cloud of bugs that left the cornfield flew toward them.

And Phillips watched the bugs in the raspberry field prepare to fly. Tens of thousands of bugs crossed the sky above them, staying out of the smoke as they circled. The hum blocked out the sound of the fires burning, the cry of the children, the low song of the women, and deep the drum beat as the young warriors stood with the sheriff, ready.

The bugs circled, dipped down, and flew back up, not quite willing to commit to the smoky air… and Phillips wondered how long before instinct overpowered caution.

They dipped into the smoke again and Phillips saw a few drop through to land directly on people. One landed on a Marine who flung the bug and wasted a pulse shot on it before his partner could smack it with a stick. A second landed on a woman by the fire and drove its ovipositor into her chest. Phillips couldn't hear her scream over the hum and he looked away as the woman stood and threw herself face forward onto the fire.

Several more bugs targeted Marines on the rooftops, and Phillips felt one man's searing pain as the bug stabbed through his body suit and implanted eggs in his knee. The man shot his own leg with the press gun, waited a moment, and everyone in the link felt the movement under his skin before he fired a second time. The pain ended in silence, and Phillips queried the man's partner only to get the image of an old-fashioned bullet hole in the silent Marine's forehead and three dead grubs trying to emerge from his leg. The partner pushed out with his own foot and the body slid off of the roof on the field side of the house.

Bugs were dropping out of the sky regularly, and just from the sheer numbers, Phillips knew they couldn't win a war of attrition. If one out of every one hundred bugs killed someone, they wouldn't last an hour.

Use the press guns from the North of the wind and keep them from getting through the smoke, he ordered and moved to the gap between two houses. The raspberry field was still crawling with bugs and he fired a shot at the darkest cluster. The new bugs took to the air and doubled the number circling.

Phillips fired a shot into the swarm as it passed his position. Hundreds of bugs fell dead as thousands continued to look for gaps in the smoke.

This isn't working, Westover sent him, and Phillips blocked the awareness of fatalities to concentrate on making his next shot count.

This really ain't working, Metzger agreed.

Suggestions? Phillips asked as he swapped out for a half-charged battery.

They sent reinforcements, Lonco said, and Phillips could see another cloud of bugs flying toward them from the South.

"Sir!" the sheriff shouted over the hum.

And Phillips turned away from the kid to assess his men, their battery supply, and the number of dead bugs.

Fire, Phillips said and pictured torching the houses.

Not enough room for everyone in the center, Lonco said.

Phillips saw a new rooftop view of the center fire pit and the people crowded around.

Sheriff? Phillips questioned Lonco when he saw himself standing next to Westover and then scanned for the group of men with clubs.

On the roofs, Weistler answered with a confirmation image of two native men on each roof, forty-three total.

The sheriff stood and threw something at the swarm of bugs as it flew past him, ignoring two bugs that tried to land on him only to be batted down by one of his friends. Just as Phillips processed the stupidity of throwing rocks at a swarm of flying bugs, the dynamite exploded and half of the bugs in that cluster were dead and raining down in pieces even as his ears registered the insult and started to ring.

Fuck me! someone shouted into the link, and Westover replied *He's all yours,* in a less than joking manner.

A second native stood and threw another stick, and Phillips didn't bother trying to plug his ears as it detonated on the edge of the diminished swarm. The surviving bugs changed path and flew toward the South.

#

"I need a radar image of the entire fucking valley," Phillips repeated to the UN Ship Captain, who seemed disappointed just to be talking to him.

"It is against regulation to ping a colony," the Captain stated again.

"We need a map of the unhatched hives so we can blow them up," Phillips argued.

"Sending current thermals," an anonymous voice said, and Metzger nodded as he watched the information load on his portable computer.

They had thermals all along, Weistler said, and Phillips didn't tell him to shut up.

The colony was reduced to five hundred children, less than two hundred women, and fifty-seven, mostly adult, men. One hundred and twenty-two

Marines were silent in his mind and Phillips had to focus constantly to block the guilt, anger, and depression that flooded the link from the surviving men, and from himself.

"Thank you," Phillips said and reached up to thumb off the communication channel.

"Be advised we are detonating located hives across the planet," the captain said and cut the line first.

"Let's go," Phillips said out loud to include the sheriff and several other locals.

Chapter 3

Projected Earth date: 2106

Planet Date: 0079, Fall

Rex Tyrol, Designated Choctaw Emigration planet, Kanto Corporation

Lt. Col. John Phillips thumbed off his radio and accepted the jar of whiskey the sheriff offered him. The alcohol muted the hot-link, and after four nights of standing watch and killing the occasional bug, Phillips wanted to pass out from exhaustion. Only his own mind kept starting to think about his command choices and how many men were gone and he would force the thoughts down, refuse to give them voice, and in controlling his own thoughts he couldn't relax enough to drift off to sleep with the other men's voices in his mind.

"Your doctor said Mike Reynolds won't survive," Sheriff Toms said as Phillips took a long swallow of the raw alcohol.

"He's just a medic; we call him Doc," Phillips said and handed the jar back to Toms. The sheriff had aged. He still didn't need to shave, but squint lines had formed around his eyes and Phillips suspected it would be a long time before the kid smiled again.

"He's all we have," Toms said after his own pull on the moonshine jar. "I checked the roster of new immigrants. Not even a vet or dentist."

"He leaves with us," Phillips said.

"I know," the sheriff replied, and the two men sat on top of a roof and drank in silence.

Phillips felt the alcohol seep into his muscles and shifted back in his chair, stretching his legs out, closing his eyes just as his radio chimed again and Metzger tried to force his thoughts through the warm haze to get his attention.

"Snows coming from the North," the sheriff commented.

"How's winters?" Phillips asked, not caring.

"We'll have six feet of snow next month. Comes in one hard storm and then stays frozen for months. The melt and flooding is just as fast. The orbital year is seven months and a few days," the sheriff explained, and Phillips let himself drift to sleep.

#

He's drunk! Westover thought as he scanned the Colonel.

Let it be, Doc. Man needs to sleep, Metzger said and gave Williams the silent order to watch over the sleeping officer.

Sixty-five Marines survived, though Westover was certain two would die from their wounds without immediate evacuation to the stasis pods on the ship in orbit. The UN Captain refused Phillips' first evacuation request, stating that the planet needed to be seventy-two hours bug-free before he would send down the shuttle. And while he suspected that Lance Corporal Trey had impregnated every fertile woman left in the colony, most of the men were working to help the local widows clean up and secure their homes.

"Sergeant Metzger," his radio echoed with the voice of the UN Ship Captain. "I am unable to reach Phillips, is there a problem?"

"Lieutenant Colonel Phillips is asleep for the first time in five days, can I help you?" Sergeant Major Metzger replied.

"I have read his report and have some questions," the man said. "Is this a secure line?"

"I am a hot-linked telepathic US Colonial Marine sharing my every thought with sixty-four other Marines and a Navy Corpsman on a rock unknown years from Earth with a current population of seven hundred and twenty-two civilians, most of whom are under the age of ten. Your ship is the only known vessel in the sky and we have no power or power station to get a signal to the single weather satellite overhead. Yeah, I think this is a secure line," Metzger said in a flat, unamused voice. "That is, if you think you can trust your side of the line," he added as an afterthought.

"Good point," the Ship Captain said and the line squealed briefly as Metzger realized the man was encrypting the transmission.

"How can I help you, Captain?" Metzger asked impatiently.

Westover stood in front of him and Metzger could feel others in the link listening.

"Your Colonel filed a formal statement that he believed that there was a native sentience on the planet," the Captain said, and Metzger felt Weistler push in his mind. The image of a moon base being shelled from orbit flooded him for a moment and he tried to focus on the radio. "Can you confirm?"

No!

No fucking way!

"Between the Pro-gen telepathy and the hot-link screwing with our senses, it's hard to say what we detected," Metzger said carefully.

"Then you do confirm detecting something unknown," the Captain said, and the line went dead with a solid click.

Fuck! Fuck! Fuck!

And Metzger was forced to close his eyes to block his own vision against the flood of panic and fear that Weistler broadcast into the link. He saw the image of himself through Weistler's eyes as the man ran toward him before Westover stepped into the other man's body and pulled him out of the link for a moment.

What the hell is going on? Phillips demanded. Weistler's panic brought him out of the alcohol-induced sleep and Metzger had the image of him dropping from the rooftop.

They are going to fucking nuke us from orbit! Weistler screamed and everyone was relieved as Westover pressed a needle against his arm and the man quickly lost consciousness.

"Report!" Phillips barked directly at Metzger and he felt himself straighten his posture on reflex.

Fucking blue hat asked for confirmation of native sentience, Sergeant Major Metzger gave a soft answer and he hung up. Then Weistler freaked the fuck out and the Doc slapped him the happy to sleep, Lonco explained. *I want some,* he added and Metzger felt his jealousy over the shot of sleep drugs.

This isn't Regent Four and the natives aren't declaring war, Phillips said as he approached Metzger, the Doc, and Weistler's unconscious form. Five Marines survived first contact with the native life-form on Regent Four, the five Marines who had been left shipboard to monitor from space during the initial landing on the technologically advanced planetoid.

Understood, Lonco said. The other Marines nodded and dropped lower in the link, going back to being aware of their own bodies.

Get him in a bed, Phillips ordered with a nod to the now-snoring Weistler.

Shuttle? someone said, and Metzger looked up with everyone else.

Bomb? someone else quipped, and Metzger studied the bright fire as it descended quickly from the clear sky.

Shuttle, Phillips said as everyone watched it descend.

Blue hat said two more days, whispered through the link.

Can't be good.

Silence, Phillips ordered and the shuttle dropped in the sky.

It took over ten minutes to go from a speck of fire to a large cargo shuttle easing itself down on thrusters, only to flip at the last moment and land on its nose in the center of the fire pit. It was a large rectangular ship with its thrusters now aimed toward the sky and rippling with heat.

The Marines formed a buffer line to keep the local children from getting close as the ship cooled down and the metal sang. The large shuttle landed precisely in the center of the rock clearing with less than ten feet between its sides and the nearest houses that circled the fire pit.

Need to buy that pilot a drink, Trey thought.

Auto-pilot, Metzger replied. *Ship's empty.*

Yeah, I get nothing, Westover added.

"This is Lieutenant Colonel John Phillips, over," Phillips said clearly into his radio, and Metzger waited, trying not to hold his breath with the other men.

The surviving colonists were gathered around, after having scrambled out of the way of the landing ship. Metzger watched them smile and joke and wait.

"This is United States Colonial Marine Lieutenant Colonel John Phillips. Answer me," Phillips said in a flat voice that carried to the civilians, and people turned to stare.

"Problem?" the sheriff asked, and Metzger saw defeat in his eyes. Saw a man who had been through hell and didn't expect good news to be real any more.

"This is Fleet Captain Liam Fu Nong of the United Nations Colony Transport ship *The Peirs Anon* to the US Colonial Marines under UN orders. You are hereby garrisoned to the Planet Rex Tyrol under the civilian charter of the Kanto Corporation until such time as a formal determination of threat can be established and verified. This planet has been declared Quarantined until the nature and severity of the local endemic fungal infection can be neutralized. The stasis chamber release codes have been sent and the landed immigrants will need immediate care. Out."

"Hot-link! We need the hot-link codes to shut down the units," Phillips shouted into the radio as Metzger stood, stunned silent, trying to process.

"Those codes are classified and sealed by the United States Marine Corps. I am not privy to them. Over."

And the line went to static.

Son of a bitch, someone said, and Metzger felt one Marine lift a handgun and pull the trigger before the full impact of being locked into the hot-link hit him.

The shot rang out and Meztger saw the civilians look around in confusion as a Marine crumpled to the ground and none of the other Marines physically reacted.

The hot-link was a simple broadcast unit fitted into the brain of each Marine, just above the left ear, that allowed the telepathic Marines to receive and broadcast other physical senses with their thoughts. Similar to the original cochlear hearing implants, but tapped into the minds perception of the senses, and able to allow one man to puppet the next in battle, if necessary.

Metzger made eye contact with Phillips and tight-beamed a questioning thought about forcing group suicide without bothering with words. The only case he knew of where a Pro-gen team hot-linked for more than seven days ended when the team went feral, hunting men on their own base. It had taken three days and over a hundred deaths before Command broadcast a shutdown code and those Marines suicided within minutes of being released from the link.

"No," Phillips answered.

Need to get inside, Westover said, moving toward the shuttle airlock.

A quick mental scan by Metzger now showed people in stasis pods, panicked and trying to get out.

"Colonel?" the sheriff asked as Metzger moved toward the shuttle and pulled his computer out to check for door codes.

"The shuttle is full of immigrants in pods, we need to get them out before people suffocate," Phillips replied, and Metzger found the codes in a message time-stamped eighteen hours previous.

"What about you?" the sheriff asked with genuine concern in his voice, and Metzger pushed down his own bitter response.

Six days was the longest that they were allowed to stay linked. It was standard protocol. Six days, and that long only because they were Marines, and Pro-gen. The suicide rate went up daily after three days, and six days was simply the longest anyone had ever survived with their sanity intact. Metzger checked his mental clock and realized that they were already six days into the link from waking.

"We get the new colonists out of those coffins and then we help you prepare for snow," Phillips said and broadcast through the link.

Chapter 4

Projected Earth date: 2132

Planet Date: 0105, Mid-Warm

Coyote's Winter House, Rex Tyrol, Designated Choctaw Emigration planet, Kanto Corporation

26 years later

"You said not Ryan," Sheila whispered.

She sat in the cemetery, North of the power plant, trying to talk to her dead mother.

Six months before, she had sat in the same place and laughed as she told her mother about Ryan, how they were getting married and then moving to his home at the Southwest Ridge camp. The Colony sat in a basin with high ridges East and West and rivers North and South. They called them the Ridge Mountains, even though they knew the true mountain was a worn down nub in the center of their clearing.

Her mother still knelt, the simple string bra turned to stone on her petrified body, the gray in her hair still glinting in the sun. She looked like a statue. All of the elders did, though few held their pose when the rot turned them to stone.

Bishop Redor was behind her, frozen in a permanent scream, the agony too much for him. Around him were the others. Most died in pain and fear, and Sheila was grateful her mother was spared the disrespect of becoming a gargoyle. Something to dare young friends to walk up to in the light of the colony's moons.

Sheila looked at the ground and then back to her mother's still form. "You told me not Ryan, now he's dead. Why?" and the hot tears spilled down her face.

An avalanche of mud and snow had down the river and across the ridge, passed their cabin, and took him away without a trace. She was a widow asking a statue why it warned her, why she was spared, why Ryan and not any of the others in the small community. She asked her mother's stone form because sometimes the dead answered. Like her mother had six months before as she was running out of the cemetery to get married. "Not Ryan," her mother had said, standing in front of her, blocking her path, solid and concerned, then a wisp of wind and she was gone.

Now Ryan was dead.

The cemetery was silent, no breeze to fuel her hopes, and Sheila stood to leave.

"Name him Jacob RunsLightly," a male voice echoed behind her.

Only no one was there, and Ryan had been sterile. They would have no children, like so many who were third generation to the planet.

Sheila sighed and started toward the cemetery gate, looking up at the spire of the shuttle ship that was now their power station.

"Name him Jacob RunsLightly," her mother said from beside her and reached a transparent hand toward Sheila's stomach.

"Why is Ryan gone? Did you kill him?" she blurted out as the spirit faded and was gone.

Only she didn't feel alone; she felt watched. From the tree line beyond the cemetery gate. She felt watched the same way she had felt watched during her entire journey back from the Southwest Ridge Camp.

Ryan was dead, the spirits of the cemetery insisted she was pregnant, and someone was following her, had been since her husband's death. Sheila gave in to the tears and the grief and the fear, sinking into the moss under the giant blue-gray hunter tree that shaded the cemetery entrance. She felt the tree's curiosity, felt someone watching her, and felt the loss of her husband add to the grief of the colony's cemetery.

The government surveyors named the planet Rex Tyrol thinking that Austria was next on the United Nations list for a planet. The immigrants from the Choctaw Nation of Mississippi called the colony Coyote's Winter House. The first few ships of colonists had been small, outposts, and when they were lost the government just kept sending new colonists in larger ships, hoping to overwhelm the planet with people until a self-sufficient colony developed.

Twice the colony was wiped out, but the government never told the new settlers, just shipped them in with more and better weapons. The second time the colony was wiped out, the resupply ship sat in orbit and monitored things, learned things. Things that were not told to the new colonists.

Then the bugs hatched again and the Marines came. Two hundred Pro-gen Colonial Marines dropped from the sky and fought the bugs, fought to protect the colonist, fought, died, and won.

When the bugs were gone from around the town, the ship in orbit off-loaded 500 new and unprepared settlers and left.

And left the Marines behind to go insane and die.

She remembered watching the few survivors bring Chief Toms' statue to the graveyard. She used to have a crush on the blond one, but he never noticed her. None of them ever looked her way; they were quiet men who scanned the tree line as they stood waiting for old man Brooks to finish talking. And then they left.

Sheila listened to the hunter tree rustle without wind and tried to stop crying.

"The skinwalker is here," the male voice whispered. Again it sounded like it was behind her, as she leaned against the tree trunk that was bigger than most houses.

"Name him Jacob RunsLightly," her mother's voice said from above her.

"The skinwalker will save him," the male voice said, still behind her.

"Smoke and fire," a third voice said, and Sheila thought that if she closed her eyes she would see the elder Peter Batton sitting beside her.

"Jacob RunsLightly, for my grandfather," her mother said.

"They are awake," a new voice said and the spirits murmured away.

Sheila sat, in silence, trying to understand the messages. The spirits rarely spoke, and she had never heard of them conversing amongst themselves before.

\#

"I'm pregnant," Sheila said as she sat in front of Dr. Westover. The doctor had landed with the Marines twenty-six years ago. He was a handsome man, in his late forties or early fifties, and her sister-in-law Patty still had a crush on him.

"Ryan-" he started to say.

"Isn't the father. He was sterile." Sheila admitted the facts without explanation because she had none. Dr. Westover knew Ryan was sterile, Ryan told her the test results before they married. Gave her the option to back out of the wedding or to request a sperm donor. She called him silly and said they would worry about children later. She had no explanation for her pregnancy because she had not slept with another man, ever. Had never been attracted to anyone available until Ryan smiled at her one day and she noticed him. And now the only thing she had to offer was the word of the spirits in the graveyard.

She sat, waiting for the doctor to say something more, but he just silently drew blood from her arm and left her alone with her thoughts while he worked his equipment and then stared at the wall.

The beep of the test brought them both back into the room.

"You're pregnant, less than a month," Dr. Westover confirmed five long minutes later. "Do you want to talk? Do you want me to treat you?" and Sheila considered the offer.

If her mother's spirit hadn't named the child, she would have accepted the abortion, rather than deal with the chance of gossip because of the timing.

Ryan hadn't told his father he was sterile, hadn't wanted to give the dying man that guilt. His father had the rot, the fungal infection that everyone eventually got on Coyote's Winter House. It was in the air, the water, the soil, and their bodies. The first infection started within years of being landed on the planet. Flu-like symptoms that got into the lungs and gave you arthritis as silica deposits built-up in unwelcome places. It killed thirty percent quickly and, for the rest, it turned from the wet, rotting decay to calcified stone as the bones dissolved before the person died. They became grotesque caricatures of who they used to be.

The second generation died young, never turned to stone, just rotted away and died, except those who didn't. Some of the second generation would fight the rot for decades until they announced their death one day, and then sat and waited as the fungus bloomed and turned them to stone. They were there one minute and a statue the next.

The third generation was usually sterile and on their way to stone from puberty. Sheila was the oldest of her generation at twenty-two in a colony of sixty-five hundred people, and everyone watched her age.

Where Ryan was sterile, Sheila had hard calcified fingernails and callouses. She used a pumice stone the way her mother used a nail file. But she wasn't sterile and now she was pregnant with a son her dead mother had named.

"Jacob RunsLightly," she said, and Dr. Westover looked up from the notes that he was pretending to study.

"I went to the cemetery and several spirits gathered around me and said his name will be Jacob RunsLightly," and for just that moment Sheila hoped the doctor would decide she was crazy and take away the pain.

"What else did they say?" he asked with more interest than Sheila expected.

Most Earth-born, first generation thought that the graveyard spirits were drunken delusions, exaggerated stories, and wish-fulfillment by grieving family members.

Sheila had told no one, not even Ryan, of her mother's first visit. Of her mother's warning.

"What else did they say?" the doctor asked again and Sheila realized she was staring into space.

"That I was pregnant. A skinwalker is awake and will save him with smoke or fire, it was all whispers and wind while I was crying," she admitted.

Dr. Westover wrote down what she said before looking up to meet her gaze and she saw his eyes shift from the hooded look of concern and analytical focus to one of the caring doctor and friend.

"Can I put down the father's name for genetic tracking?" he asked, pen back to notes.

"I don't know," was her only answer.

#

"A skinwalker?" Jessup Tranger asked, interrupting Westover again.

"That's what she said," the doctor agreed.

Jessup Tranger was the elected Chief of the Peoples. The power station was built with the shell of a colony shuttle, two blast craters from previous colony ships framed the town and gave them a clear field of fire West and Southwest of the town. The ridge stretched across the West and the graveyard marked the start of the giant impenetrable forest that grew to the edge of the cold river that spanned the globe. The orbital survey of the planet had revealed frozen lakes but no oceans, and three giant rivers that meandered around the ridges that were all that remained of ancient mountains, and then through the forests, pulled by the three moons that dictated the planetary weather.

"That's tribal, right? It's a ghost?" the doctor asked as they moved to the entrance of the cemetery.

"No. Yes." Jessup started, as his gaze searched the graveyard for motion. "It's a shape-shifter, like a werewolf. Weird."

"I don't think she was lying. She believes the ghosts talked to her," the doctor said without mentioning the pregnancy. "They told her that the skinwalker is awake and would save someone with smoke or fire."

"Weird," Jessup Tranger said again.

Neither man was quite willing to enter the graveyard. The grotesque dead could be seen clearly from the entrance and the dark hunter tree had pulled in its leaves and lower branches for the night, making it impossible to move past without getting close to a man's statue that was beginning to crumble from the weather. His single hand, reached out, blocking the side of the path, lower jaw broken off, the wrinkles of pain stretching down into his neck with his face pointed toward the cloudy sky.

"What did the Peters kid say?" Jessup asked as he turned his back on the graveyard in favor of the view of the power station.

"His grandfather's ghost told him that 'they are awake, don't play in the vines," he repeated.

"It's got to be the bugs," Jessup said, walking away from the graveyard.

"We have another year before a hatching is due," the doctor protested. "But, skinwalker, they burrow in you, do you believe in the ghosts?"

"Spirits. The spirits of our elders have always come to us with messages. Even on Earth," Jessup said slowly as a man appeared in front of them. The wind shifted lightly and the spirit drifted with the breeze.

"The skinwalker will save you," the spirit said in a whisper.

"The bugs-" Jessup started to say but a violent gust of icy wind cut him off on the already cold day.

"The skinwalker will save you. They need to." And the spirit was gone to dust on the breeze in the dusk.

"The bugs," Westover said without being willing to say what he was afraid of.

"No, I think he meant the Marines," Jessup corrected. He was unwilling to move from where the contact had happened, hoping for another message. Hoping for clarification.

"Are there any left?" Jessup asked, but Westover was gone.

Chapter 5

Projected Earth date: 2132

Planet Date: 0105, Mid-Warm

Coyote's Winter House, Rex Tyrol, Designated Choctaw Emigration planet, Kanto Corporation

"Jeff says they never found his body," Patty said as she poured two cups of tea.

Sheila stared into the depth of her cup, the lavender-colored tea was made from the hunter trees' sprouts. The energy boost wasn't caffeine, it gave a clear head and calmed fear and panic, and people had been trying to give it to her ever since Ryan's death. She never liked the flavor and pretended to sip, politely.

"The flood ground the hunter trees to a pulp. A piece of the ridgeline is just gone," she repeated the facts without emotion. "He couldn't outrun it and he didn't survive it. Ryan is dead." Saying it again still didn't make it real for her.

"Jeff said he never saw the water hit Ryan," Patty said, and Sheila knew she wanted to hope that her brother was still alive.

"He couldn't survive the water, Patty," Sheila said and reached out to stop her sister-in-law from topping up the little she'd drunk as the other woman refilled her own cup.

Patty sighed, took a long drink of her own hot tea, and pushed a plate of small, fried cookies toward Sheila.

"I used sweet lime," Patty said, without enthusiasm. The colony had limited access to sweeteners; beets and cane didn't survive the short growing seasons and bees never survived a year past landing. Sweet lime was a crystalized sugar alcohol that settlers collected from the sand bars once a planetary year when the temperature got high enough to evaporate the pools of water the native squids created for hunting the flutterbys. It tasted like citric lime and vinegar and was sweet enough to bake with, while difficult enough to harvest to make it a treat.

"Thank you," Sheila said without conviction as her imagination supplied an image of Ryan washed up on the riverbank and the native squids swarming his battered body.

The cookie was moist and sweet and the sour flavor was masked by cherry and anise. Sheila forced herself to take a second cookie and smile before faking another sip of her lukewarm tea.

"Jeff says you visited Doctor Westover today, are you okay?" Patty asked and ate a cookie herself.

Sheila wanted to tense up, wanted to say something bitter about her sister-in-law's need to use her husband as an excuse to pry. Wanted to walk away from the self-centered woman and never look back. But in a colony of six thousand, the Southwest Ridge Camp was the farthest, most isolated place to go. The forest was close to impenetrable. Where one hunter tree could be spoken to or bypassed, the forest was a tight mixture of hungry hunter trees and poisonous silver grass.

"Jeff says-"

"I'm pregnant," Sheila cut her off and waited for the other woman to process. She was not expecting the hug that engulfed her, spilling both cups of tea and scattering the cookies.

"Oh, honey! Ryan knew the two of you would beat the odds," Patty said after she pulled back, dried her tears, and then wiped enthusiastically at the spilled tea that was dripping onto the floor for Ryan's dog to lap up.

Sheila hadn't been able to make herself face Nillie, the golden retriever she and Ryan were forced to leave with his sister when they accepted the spot at the camp. Nillie was five years old and the rot was already starting on his shoulders and forelegs. Sheila slid off of the kitchen chair and gently embraced the dog, who turned to lick her face with a lime-scented tongue.

The tears came fast and Sheila sat on the kitchen floor next to the dog, wanting to bury her face in the dog's fur but knowing that the rot was painful and not wanting to hurt the old boy.

"Wait until I tell Jeff," Patty said from someplace above her. "I'm going to be an auntie!"

And Sheila decided that no one but she and the doctor needed to know that Ryan tested sterile before they married. It was no one's business and no one would ever know except her son. And his father.

#

"Stupid, stupid, stupid," Westover muttered as he made his way along the safe path through the silver grass to his small, isolated cabin on the edge of Crater Lake.

Don't you ever think?

He told her he was sterile.

Of course he told her, stupid lovers.

What were you thinking?

Did she consent?

She was lonely.

So you stuck a dick in her?

You saw her.

"Why doesn't she remember?" he asked the empty field, and a single flutterby moved on the breeze to check him out.

The flutterby's iridescent air sack deflated slightly so that it could drop onto the path in front of Westover, and he paused to stare at the creature that had become familiar in the twenty-six years since being stranded on the planet.

It was small for a flutterby, the size of a large pumpkin, more than half its form was the air sack that allowed it to float on the breeze, and it had a flesh body and brain that was nearly transparent in the fading sunlight. A rim of gauzy frill encircled its body and fluttered rapidly to move it against a breeze if needed. Mostly they floated, eating microscopic bugs in the air and avoided the trees, people, and anything else near them. Sometimes they played keep-away with children and dogs.

Just kick it.

Westover waited, silent, as the sun dropped lower and the breeze turned bitter.

When the indigenous animal finally re-inflated itself and drifted off on the breeze; he was greeted by a large puddle of steaming green ooze that blocked his path.

Fuck!

He moved to squeeze between the shit and the deadly silver grass that seemed to reach out toward him. He realized that he couldn't clear the grass safely and took a moment to assess his options.

His cabin was in front of him, less that twenty yards away. He closed his eyes and opened the link fully to see the North river glinting in the sunset, some teenagers laughing as they walked by without glancing at him. The power station to the west, a Frankenstein building that was created with the shuttle at its heart and surrounded by the few buildings that made up the town square, the shuttle's exhaust turrets three stories higher than anything else and reflecting the purple sunset. A window looking into a dark, empty bedroom from across a field. The power station from the South, shadows stretching across green wheat fields toward the stream. A campfire, small, with a chicken cooking on a spit.

It's not poisonous.

He took a deep breath, to pull himself from the link and calm his frustration, and then fastidiously stepped on the shallow puddle and walked toward his cabin, scraping his left shoe every few steps.

#

Her mother's cabin was empty and cold as Sheila entered. There was a dampness to the air and she moved from room to small room, lighting lamps and candles. The blower on her wood stove stuttered twice before she heard the motor stabilize. She had a moment of bitter pleasure when she went into her old room and it was exactly as she left it.

Her mother died two months before Sheila married Ryan and as many people encouraged them to take over the cabin as tried to insist that she sell it. Ryan held her hand when she lied and told her cousins that they planned to move back into it when they returned from the camp. They had never planned to return, but she wasn't ready to box up her mother's life and put her childhood into storage.

She and Ryan made love on her bed, locked up the cabin, and walked away together to start their new life.

Now she was back, sitting on her bed, wishing she had brought Nillie with her, and trying not to give in to the tears.

An hour passed and the guttering of the candle brought her back to the room. Sheila stood up and moved around the house again, blowing out candles and turning down the lamps. The house was still cold despite the fan that she could hear faintly, and Sheila knelt and placed her hand against a vent to confirm the warmth blowing slowly into the room. She turned one lamp back up and walked from the main room to the

kitchen to see that the back door window was open
again. Her mother always insisted that she was going to
fix the broken lock one day. Sheila remembered
arguing that the window needed to be fixed because of
the threat of the bugs, and her mother would chide that
she would be dead and stone before the bugs returned.

Sheila closed the window and wedged a bit of
curtain into the sill to keep it from working open easily.

Walking back to her room, Sheila felt watched
again. She sat on her bed, thought about getting
undressed, and settled for turning the lamp down and
laying back on top of her covers. She didn't have the
energy to get up and shake out the covers, and she was
unwilling to climb between sheets that had sat in an
empty house with a window open for eight months.
With her shoes still on, she curled up in a ball and cried
herself to sleep.

He held her, his warmth seeped into her back
and the pain faded a little. His hand slid around her
body and she expected him to slide it down into her
pants and stroke her until she relaxed and let him pull
her pants down. The dream was familiar. It came every
night since Ryan's death. Only tonight, he didn't reach
between her legs. Tonight he held her with one hand on
her still flat stomach. Sheila drifted in the arms of her
dream lover and tried to wake up. Tried to tell him she
was pregnant. But he was warm and he was strong, and
his breath on her neck calmed her fears. And tonight he
fell asleep.

#

The sun was shining through her window, Sheila could hear children playing outside, and the stove fan was quiet.

She laid in bed and tried to recapture the warmth of her dream. She slid her hand across the bed beside her and was startled by a sharp line of warm-to-cold bedding where someone had lain beside her. She sat upright. Ran her hands on either side of her, and then stared at the pillow and the single strand of Ryan's short brown hair that was caught on a pillow button.

And she felt someone watching her. She thought she should be frightened, thought she should be angry, but instead she felt safe.

The dream lover had come every night since Ryan's death and that eliminated anyone from the main town. The dream lover came last night and Sheila knew Jeff and the rest of the Southwest Ridge Camp crew had left the day before.

The dream lover was an ancestor, one of the spirits, she realized. That's why they took an interest in her child and named him for her.

"Jacob RunsLightly," she said out loud and started cleaning the small cabin that was now hers.

Chapter 6

Projected Earth date: 2132

Planet Date: 0105, Mid-Warm

Coyote's Winter House, Rex Tyrol, Designated Choctaw Emigration planet, Kanto Corporation

"Problem, Chief?" Beth Pyle asked from the top of the spiral staircase.

Chief Jessup Tranger stood on the Northwest lookout platform and studied the Peters' grape vineyard with night vision goggles on infrared. The field was a uniform green, not even a flutterby in sight.

"Evening, Sheriff. Joey Peters visited his grandson today," Jessup said without turning or looking away from the field.

"Christ!" Beth said and moved to stand behind him, her breath on his left arm as he continued to scan the vineyard.

"Yeah, his mother fainted. Kid told Westover that his grandfather said 'They are awake, don't go in the vines.' I don't see anything," and he lowered the goggles.

"Why were they at the cemetery?" Beth asked and slid under Jessup's arm to look over the railing at the lit path below.

"They weren't. Westover said they were at Fallsbreak Park."

"I don't like him," Beth said in a casual voice as Jessup moved to embrace her in front of him while they both watched the small yellow moon drift through the clouds. The red moon was down for another few days and the brown moon was low to the trees.

"Westover? Yeah, he's a weird one. Getting old," Jessup said and left it at that.

"Kim Bailey said there was a spirit at the power plant today," Beth said. "She said it never spoke, just drifted around touching dials for a minute and then was gone."

"Christ," Jessup said softly and lifted the goggles back up to scan the grapes again.

"Maybe the raspberry vines by the Power station?" Beth offered.

"Christ."

\#

The first dawn came before Jessup was ready to wake up, and he silently cursed forgetting to close the curtain the night before as the sunlight hit the brown moon and turned it blindingly golden from the ice in its atmosphere. He shifted carefully, so as not to wake up his fiancé, Beth, and pulled the blanket up to cover his face. Beth protested in her sleep and turned away from him, taking the blanket with her.

Naked, cold, and half-blinded, Jessup sat up and scanned the room for his clothes.

"Take Kim some tobacco and sage," Beth muttered from under the blanket ten minutes later when he returned from washing up and relieving himself. He glanced about her room looking for his C&C.

Jessup smiled, wondering if it was a real request or if she was talking in her sleep.

He thought about kissing her goodbye, but the blanket never moved, and he made his way to her kitchen quietly.

"Hey, Chief," Beth's younger brother Alec said from behind a large bowl of hot, cooked grains. He was reading another old notebook and Jessup made a note to himself to dig out the box of old Chief's journals from the back of his office for the kid.

"Hey, Alec, any coffee?" Jessup replied.

"Yeah, on the stove." Alec nodded his head toward the old clay rocket stove and the pot on the back ledge.

It wasn't real coffee; the plant didn't tolerate the planet's short growing season. It was a mixture of roasted grains and native caffeine that the first generation colonists hated and the second generation tolerated.

"Thanks," Jessup said and opened the cupboard with the cups without asking.

Alec continued to eat his breakfast, reading, without comment.

"You going fishing today?" Jessup asked after he filled his cup.

"Yeah. The Crater Lake Moogies are getting rude, thought we'd drop a few booms and see what's for dinner," Alec said, setting the notebook down carefully.

And for a moment Jessup wanted nothing more than to skip the power plant, not worry about spirits giving warnings, and go fishing like he was still just one of the guys. Wanted to walk away from being elected chief of the colony at age thirty-two, forget that he only had five to ten years left before the fungus that was eating his left foot's toenails bloomed in his body, pretend he wasn't an elder in a colony with a male life expectancy of just forty years. He thought about calling up Jacob Waits, his deputy chief, and telling the first generation nancy to go to the power station for him.

But Jacob Waits was only three years on the planet and still didn't think he would get the rot, thought that being born and raised on Earth meant he was smarter. Didn't believe in the spirits or even the bugs. Liked to spout off how the Corporation wouldn't risk its investment in him. Bragged about how much he received for selling out his treaty rights and emigrating.

And spent that emigration money paying to ship twenty-four breeding sheep to the colony. And trinkets to buy votes. He brought those, too.

"Beth said there was tobacco and sage for Kim Bailey?" Jessup asked as he finished his second bitter cup, not willing to use his fiancé's sweet lime or cream.

"No clue, Chief, try the out box," Alec answered, still eating the gruel as if it tasted good and glancing down at the notebook page.

Jessup moved to the kitchen door and looked into the wooden box on the table. A cloth wrapped bundle sat in the box and he picked it up, untying the corners of the cloth and confirmed that it contained a bag of dried leaf tobacco and a sage bundle tied with a red thread.

"Be careful, today," Jessup said to Alec, looking at him long enough for the teen to look up from his reading. "Something's up."

"The spirits are restless," Alec agreed, and Jessup found himself swallowing against a dry throat.

"What have you heard?" Jessup asked, trying to sound casual after his own ominous warning.

"There was one at the school yesterday. Joey said it told the teacher to lock the door and burn sage," Alec replied and went back to reading.

"Put the word out. I need to know what the elders are telling people; they can message my office," Jessup said and turned to leave.

"You got it, Chief."

#

"What is it, boy?" Patty asked as she walked into the kitchen.

Nillie sat by the door, staring intently at a point across from the cook stove, and whimpered, his tail trying to wag against the pain of the seeping wound on his back.

The rot now spread from his front shoulders to cover his back, and Patty raised her hand to her mouth in shock.

"Oh baby," she said, trying not to cry, and sank to the floor in front of her brother's dog. Nillie was the only live birth of his litter, and she and Ryan took turns nursing him. Five years was old for a dog on the colony and Patty knew it was coming, but to lose Nillie so soon after Ryan was breaking her heart.

Nillie shifted slightly and stared at a spot behind her. The dog's moist eyes, happy for the first time in weeks.

"Fat ass," her father's voice said, and Patty froze, staring at Nillie who gave out a small yip of joy.

"Leave us alone," the voice said, and Patty recognized his tone. He had spoken that way to her when her kitten got in the silver grass. And he said the exact same thing when her older brother realized that the rot was about to kill him at only twenty-three. He told her to leave and he sat with the dying, and now he was ordering her to leave Nillie to die.

Patty struggled to her feet, looked at the empty spot Nillie was staring at, patted the dog on the head once, and ran from the house crying in her slippers and robe.

#

"Halito," Kim Bailey called out as Jessup climbed off of his scooter.

"Hey, Kim," he replied. "Beth sent you some tobacco and sage," and he offered the small bundle to his fiancé's cousin.

"Thanks," Kim replied. "You going fishing?"

"No, I'm here on business," Jessup said and followed her into the cannibalized shuttle's airlock.

"Oh, Beth told you about our visitor yesterday? I swear I wasn't drinking," Beth said with a light laugh as she opened the interior door and walked across the cargo bay toward the control station on the far side of the shuttle.

"You weren't the only one they visited," Jessup replied as they waited for Ross Senhass to buzz the door and let them in to the control room.

"Hey, Ross! Wake up!" Kim shouted into the intercom before pulling out her computer and sending the junior engineer a message.

The door gave a click and Jessup pulled it open.

Inside, seventeen-year-old Ross Senhass was rubbing one eye while staring around the room in confusion. A thin layer of dust coated every surface and more was still sifting out of the air.

"I swear, I didn't fall asleep, Chief," Ross said when he saw Jessup behind Kim. "I made my four am checks and then Kim was yelling at me. I've never fallen asleep before," Ross continued to explain, and

Jessup held up one hand to quiet him while watching the older Kim make a circuit of the room, checking gauges and screens.

"Everything looks good," Kim finally said. "Except the dust; that's going to get into things bad."

"I never fell asleep," Ross started again, and Jessup felt sorry for the youth. Kim had trained under an Earth-born engineer from the time she was old enough to follow her mother to work. Ross was late to the game and was training under Kim.

"Spirits," Kim said, more to herself, Jessup thought.

"I had a dream!" Ross blurted out. "Three spirits built a fire in the Main line and told me to keep it hot to light the way."

Jessup and Kim stared at the other man.

"A fire in the Main line would melt the shuttle," Kim said in a quiet voice.

"It was a weird dream, there were wolves hunting just outside the fire, and a tree growing up from the flames only its branches had the rot and something was eating the roots," Ross spoke quickly, and his voice trailed off.

"Was there anything else?" Jessup asked before Kim could discourage her coworker.

"There were three spirits, one was a hunter tree, one was a flutterby, and one was an elder but I couldn't see who," Ross said slowly, and Jessup thought about asking Kim to leave before her pained expression discouraged him.

"And?" Jessup prompted.

"The flutterby turned toward me, with the fire behind it and then they all shifted to make room for me by the fire," Ross said with closed eyes.

"And?" Jessup prompted again.

"Kim was on the intercom and I was standing right here in a cloud of dust," Ross said with a shrug.

Chapter 7

Projected Earth date: 2132

Planet Date: 0105, Mid-Warm

Coyote's Winter House, Rex Tyrol, Designated Choctaw Emigration planet, Kanto Corporation

"Jacob! Jacob!" Patty shouted as she opened the school house door and stood on the threshold. It was still too early for the kids to be there but she knew Jacob Waits liked to arrive early and use the station computer for his writing. "Jacob!" she shouted again, not leaving the doorway as she twisted to stare back toward her cabin.

The small school, the colony administration building, and the hospital were built in a cluster beside the grounded shuttle that was their power station, allowing for electricity and better computers than the C&C's everyone carried. The handheld computer and communication units, were pocket-sized and the first generation colonist called them cell phones even though they were only radios with a built-in link to the station computer.

"Jacob!" Patty almost screamed, still watching her cabin across the school's stickball field.

"Problem?" Jacob asked from the North side of the building as he jogged toward her.

He was slightly overweight, with a rounded brown face. He had short, black hair hidden under the baseball cap that covered his bald spot with its brightly embroidered Kanto Corp logo. He had arrived in the last colonist drop three years ago with freeze-dried yeast, Russian wheat seeds that handled the weather, and mean mountain sheep for wool. He also brought new encyclopedia files for the school and a box of real books to add to the colony library. And a Colt .357 that he wore on his hip, even though few in the colony bothered to carry sidearms that were ineffective against the local dangers.

Patty had campaigned for him.

"My dad is with Nillie; he has the rot real bad," Patty said and moved toward her cabin, expecting Jacob to follow.

The newcomer stood at the walk and wiped his face with a white cloth.

"You said your dad was dead," he commented, and Patty spun back toward him in anger at the doubt and blandness of his voice.

"My dad's spirit is with my dog, come on!" she snapped with an edge of hysteria in her voice.

"Where?" Chief Jessup Tranger asked from the path to the South of the school, and Patty looked up to see Ross Senhass standing beside him, looking shook-up and about as upset as she felt.

"My cabin!" Patty exclaimed and turned to hurry back to her kitchen and the scene she'd fled earlier.

#

"Hey! Check it out!" Toni shouted and pointed out across the field of silver grass, toward the edge of the hunter tree forest.

Alec and the others turned to look in time to see a single large flutterby desperately fighting to stay above the razor sharp tips of the poisonous silver grass. Flutterbys looked like jellyfish, but Alec knew they were more closely related to the squid-like creatures that inhabited the waters. They floated by, capturing their own gas in an organic cellophane bag that they blew after eating sweet lime. Alec usually ignored them, being one of the few things on the planet not trying to kill him.

"What's its problem?" Loko asked as the creature bobbed closer and closer to them, dropping to within inches of the deadly grass before settling on the path in front of them.

"Fuck, man! It's going to shit on our path," Toni protested.

"It's got the rot," Moko said, pointing at the telltale slick infection on the side where the air sack joined to its nearly transparent body. The green-black fungus could be seen inside its body, obscuring most of its organs and half of its brain.

"Damn! Never heard of that before!" Alec exclaimed.

"Somebody film it!" Toni said excitedly.

"Got it," Loko said and held his C&C up as a camera.

"Jessup!" Alec activated his own C&C, but the line toned out and then Jessup's calm voice offered options for leaving a message. "Fuck," Alec said and thumbed the unit off.

The flutterby was visibly deflating in front of them. The air sack seemed to grow brittle and they all jumped when it tore free with a popping sound and was carried away on the wind.

"I found an air sack yesterday, down by the South creek," Moko offered and Loko nodded, not taking his camera off of the dying creature.

"Thought a hunter tree missed," Loko added.

Alec tried Jessup's number again as the flutterby started making a high-pitched whine, like a motor running too hot, and the chief's answering message restarted. The creature shimmered as the fungus bloomed and completely covered its form.

The boys stood, looking at the now blackish-green creature that was almost two feet across and dead center on the path. The wet fungus dried quickly and blew away as dust on the breeze, leaving a large, familiar-looking boulder.

"Fuck me," Toni said, staring at the boulder that was nearly identical to the thousands of similar rocks that colonists used to mark paths and boundaries.

"Sweet," Alec agreed.

Nothing about the boulder suggested that it was a flutterby. It was now one of the coarse, tuff-like rocks that littered the landscape; everything flutterby was inside the shell.

#

"We good, Chief?" Ross asked as Jessup moved to follow Patty.

"Yes," Jessup replied. "You might want to see this," he said to Jacob Waits.

The other man looked from the shaken-up Ross to Jessup before giving an exasperated sigh and moving to follow Patty.

Jessup heard the dog's whines before they were halfway across the stickball field.

Westover was standing in the open doorway, watching something inside the kitchen, and Jessup watched Patty run up and Westover block her from entering.

Jessup and Jacob arrived at the kitchen door and Jessup leaned a bit to see past Patty and into the room.

The golden retriever sat, staring at something in front of it and dripping in black fungal slime.

Jessup winced in sympathy, most humans were writhing and screaming by the time the rot bloomed to cover them.

"Sweet Jesus, do something!" Jacob Waits blurted out when he caught a glimpse of the dog, and Jessup turned to see him backing away.

"You got a gun," was Westover's only comment as the doctor moved away from the doorway and the whines of the dog.

"No!" Patty protested and an icy gust of wind hit them from the North.

"The skinwalker waits," a male voice echoed from inside the cabin before Jacob could reach for his weapon.

Jessup put his hand on Jacob's arm and shook his head with a hard stare.

"Who was that?" Jacob demanded, staring around the kitchen and then turning to face Jessup.

"A spirit," Jessup replied.

"My father," Patty answered, watching the same spot the dog was staring at.

"Don't give me any of that medicine-man mumbo," Jacob said with a snort and turned back toward the kitchen door.

"You abandoned your culture; your ancestors didn't abandon you," Jessup said in a soft, angry voice.

It was the continuation of an argument that every second-generation colonist had with the new arrivals. The corporation shipped in a transport every five years with five hundred warm bodies and a few needed supplies. People who had sold their treaty rights for the promise of a new beginning. Their children grew up with spirits in the cemetery that would talk, give advice or warnings, and occasionally dance to the drums when all three moons where in the sky. The second generation reread the old stories and reconnected with everything their parents left behind. The third generation died young and there was no fourth generation, yet. Sheila was pregnant.

The dog let out one last pained howl and then was quiet.

"Damn," Jacob said and Jessup thought he might be disappointed that he wouldn't get to shoot the animal.

"Five minutes," Westover said, blocking Patty from entering.

"What the hell's a skinwalker? Are you telling me that dog is going to be a werewolf?" Jacob demanded of Jessup and Patty stopped crying to turn and stare.

"The spirits have been saying a skinwalker is coming and warning us for days," Jessup replied, thinking that a dog spirit might explain things.

"Bullshit superstitions. I should have known," Jacob said and spun and walked away.

"He's trouble," Westover said, his arm still around Patty's shoulder.

"Wooof," whispered on the wind and Jessup felt dog fur brush his hand.

Patty looked around as the breeze blew dust devils on the path.

#

"Ryan always said Nillie was special," Patty said as she poured raw alcohol into her cup of tea. "Said he would have been a Pro-gen dog on Earth."

Westover sat and watched the woman process through her shock. The dog still sat, staring intently at someone, only now he was stone, yellow highlights glinting on his shoulders and haunches.

Patty was beautiful and he wished she wasn't sterile. Wished she wasn't so emotionally broken. On Earth, a single dose of nanos would have corrected her neural paths and given her a chance. Here, it was all he could do to keep her focused and out of the deep end.

"Do you want some tea?" Patty asked again, and Westover shook his head no, letting her talk her way through the pain.

"Ryan should have been here. Sheila says his body was lost. Jeff says he's part of the river now. Do you think you can be a spirit without becoming a statue?" she asked while absentmindedly wiping the fungal dust from the table and counter. As she turned away from Westover, he saw a wet stain under her pajama top, running from her left shoulder down to the tucked-in edge at her waist band.

"How's your shoulder?" Westover asked in a quiet voice.

Patty turned to look at him with a blank stare and several blinks before she processed the question. Her right hand reached up and over to touch a spot above her left shoulder blade gently.

"It's not that big, it's just wet. I drink so much. Do you think it's the tea? Or the alcohol?" She went back to wiping off the fungus spores that the dog shed in transition.

"The tea is good for you. Let me know when you want something stronger," Westover said and stood to leave. "I'll let Sheila know to come over," he added and moved to the door.

Patty never looked up from her task and Westover watched her use the blackened towel to push the dust around before he sighed and left.

#

How old is she? The question hit as soon as Westover got clear of the cabin and onto the empty path, heading toward Sheila's cabin in the next cluster of houses.

The colony was holding at a population of six thousand four hundred, mostly scattered in twenty- to forty-house groups, in circles moving away from the shuttle power. The first colony landing blasted a safe zone to the North and set up camp, but the giant trees were far more flexible than their first generation minds planned for and that colony abandoned the cabins closest to the forest.

When the power station was blown only a crescent moon of cabins survived the blast. None of the colonists survived the bugs. The second colonists also placed their power station shuttle against the trees. Its crater was deeper, but no one was willing to live in their empty cabins. The third wave of colonists placed their shuttle far from the first two, along the main river. When the Marines came, they shut it down while fighting the bugs. Only an unseasonable rain came and the bugs used the river to take the shuttle and two hundred occupied houses with it.

Now the latest shuttle sat atop the rocks at the center of the basin.

Lonco shot a bunch of defects. Pro-gen isn't perfect.

The dog.

I can hear it.

Call it.

Westover stopped walking and looked around to make certain he was still alone. The image of himself standing on the path, looking around in confusion flooded him, and he frowned and started walking again.

Twenty-one, third generation, echoed through him. *Dump the sperm.*

#

Jessup walked from the stickball field toward the raspberry vine field to the North. Kids were arriving at the school and he was glad that Jacob would be busy for the rest of the day.

A faint growl came from in front of him and he stopped to listen. The dog spirit shifted the breeze directly in front of him with a faint outline and then growled again. Low in its throat, a warning to something.

Jessup scanned the raspberries on either side of the path. The vines were full of fruit, just starting to shift from green to pink and red in places and Jessup knew people were sneaking into the field, looking for the occasional early fruit.

There were three medium-sized flutterbys above the field to the left of the path and one, small, to the right. Jessup took another step and the dog spirit never shifted. Standing beside the spirit, Jessup could see a patch of vines thirty yards into the field row that looked brown. He started to move off of the path to check it out, but the dog spirit barked loudly and was gone.

"Moths to a flame," a man's voice said from beside him.

Jessup didn't bother to look to see if the spirit was recognizable; it was his brother's voice.

"Talk to me, Joey, no riddles," Jessup said softly.

"Light a fire, they see heat, you need more time," and the breeze pulled the spirit apart.

Chapter 8

Projected Earth date: 2132

Planet Date: 0105, Mid-Warm

Coyote's Winter House, Rex Tyrol, Designated
Choctaw Emigration planet, Kanto Corporation

"He loved the garden," Patty said, and Sheila
knew it was a lie. Nillie loved digging in the garden,
loved chewing on the horseradish leaves, and loved the
occasional flutterby that drifted over the garden. But
Nillie hated being locked in the garden and would bark
until one of the neighbor kids unlatched the gate and let
him run loose. He stayed on the paths, visited anyone
who was cooking, and always made his way to the
school and the kids playing stickball.

"It's a good place for him," Sheila said,
struggling to balance the stone dog as Patty glanced
around looking for a spot. Nillie still weighed almost
the same as he had alive, 60 pounds of porous stone.

"By the horseradish, so he can watch the gate," she offered.

"Oh, perfect," Patty said and the two women set the dog down carefully. "Would you like some tea?"

#

"Hey, Chief," Alec said and nodded his head toward Jessup.

The older man was approaching silently from the edge of the trail, risking hunter tree branch fingers to try and sneak up on the four guys. Alec was the oldest at eighteen, the twins Loko and Moko were a few months younger than him and still seventeen, and Toni was tolerated, being a mature fifteen. Toni was third generation and Alec let him tag after him since the kid was three years to Alec's almost seven. Most third gens died by twelve, but Toni was healthy and showed no sign of the rot. The older boys did tease him about the fine grain gravel he occasionally shed as dandruff.

"Chief's here!" Alec called out to make sure Toni hid his beer before Jessup turned the corner. Alec didn't need to look to see if Toni had a beer, it was there, Toni was there, and he just didn't feel like a new lecture on being responsible because he was oldest.

His sister, Beth, teased that he was in line to be chief, and Alec was chafing at the idea.

"I'll take one of those beers," Chief Jessup Tranger said and Alec almost fell off his boulder.

"Beers?" Alec asked, masking his emotions quickly as he fiddled with the fuse on a small blasting primer.

The hunter trees got angry if you used anything bigger than 50 grains, and Alec had enough problems with the trees ever since Pete Langer dared him to piss on one in fifth grade. No one ever listened to him in the colony, but the trees knew he was the kid one of them caught to eat but who escaped by blowing a blasting cap off. The trees blamed him for the fact that, ever since his escape, colonists all carried a blasting cap against capture. The trees remembered and didn't let him pass where others could walk freely. The trees and he had established a bit of a truce just six months ago, when he started shooting the undomesticated pigs that ran wild on the edges of the forest and dug up the hunter tree roots and ruined the colony's crops. And for the first time since fifth grade, the trees grudgingly let him move about the colony without harassing or threatening him. The day after he threw the carcass of a pig to a hunter tree by the South river, they quit pushing at him.

But no one ever listened to him about the trees, and Jessup could report him for the beer he snuck out for his friends, so Alec kept a neutral face as he primed a second blast.

"Christ!" Jessup said with tired exasperation as he sank onto the boulder beside Alec and reached for a blasting primer to set for fishing. "Don't tell me I walked all the way out here to sneak a beer for nothing." The chief handed back a tightly fixed primer.

"Here, Chief," Toni said, and Alec could have slapped his forehead as the kid handed Jessup his own nearly full beer. "Tastes like shit," Toni replied to Alec's expression and gave a simple shrug.

Jessup drank the bottle of lukewarm beer in one long, head-back swallow, before lowering the bottle with a nod that seemed to communicate that the beer had fixed something.

"Your nets ready?" was the chief's only comment as Alec handed him a second beer from his stash behind his boulder.

"The twins are tying rope now," Alec answered. Catching a moogie was as simple as lassoing a cat, and the nets they used were stretched across a loop of heavy rope that was attached to a long, sturdy pole with a sharpened point. The net and lasso detached from the pole easily and the spears were also used for getting clams out of their nests when there were no moogies around. "I tried to call you," he added after Jessup drank half of the second bottle.

"You're sitting on a flutterby," Toni said proudly and handed the C&C over with the video from earlier already keyed to play.

#

"Mr. Waits," a small child asked from his office doorway and Jacob worked to calm his annoyance before smiling at the child. Eight-year-old Martin Cosery was not one to bother him; usually he was one to be drug in by an angry teacher demanding punishment of the unrepentant kid.

"Yes?" Jacob finally prompted when the child stood, not speaking, in his doorway for several minutes and the sounds of the other children leaving school for the day faded away.

"Will you walk me home?" the boy asked with sad, blinking eyes that didn't ask for sympathy.

Jacob switched off his desk computer as he stood, without checking to see if his file was saved, and was walking toward the doorway and the distressed child.

"Sure, Mart, let me grab my coat. Where's your coat?" Jacob cursed the fact that at no point in the school day had anyone noticed the bruised look about the boy's eyes or the tremor in his voice.

"I don't have it," Martin said quietly as Jacob steered toward the boy's classroom.

Ell Menedez was still in the room, straightening things up, and Jacob saw her glance at the boy and then pause to actually look at him.

"Your mom isn't here, yet?" she asked in a forced voice that told Jacob she was just realizing that she had missed something.

"No, ma'am. Mr. Waits said he would walk me home," the boy answered and then turned his tired gaze up to give Jacob a hero-worship look.

"Mart, could you sweep for Ms. Menedez while I talk to her, and then we can get going," Jacob asked and ruffled the boy's hair.

Any other time the kid would have told him to fuck off and spat on his shoe, today he froze for a moment and then walked quietly to get the broom from the back of the room.

"He came in at lunch and never said anything. I thought he might have a cold," the teacher said softly, not waiting for the question.

Jacob nodded.

"Why didn't he walk home with his brother Tommy?" she continued and then froze, hand to mouth in a gesture so stereotypical that Jacob almost laughed.

"Call Sheriff Bethany Pyle; tell her what little we know. It isn't much. Have her check out the boy's house and call me. I'm taking him home with me," Jacob said and watched the teacher process the situation.

"Do you think…" but she couldn't bring herself to finish the question.

"He would have brought his brother to school with him if it was just the mom. Tell Beth to take Mister Westover, just in case, and call the chief," Jacob said quickly and nodded to the boy as he finished sweeping and turned to watch them talking.

#

"Sweet!" Toni shouted when the first blasting cap went off in the lake with a muted thump. Then he scrambled back from the bank as a mid-sized moogie jumped from the water to barely miss him. The creature was a round ball of gelatinous ooze that shot out three long tentacle-like arms to snare the boy's legs.

Jessup threw a primer at the twenty-pound moogie and watched with a smile as it detonated and the static shock killed the animal. The bag of ooze was discolored from ruptured organs, and they left it on the shore for the feral cats to find later.

"Shit!" Toni said as a second, smaller moogie, shot out of the water and hit him in the side, the gelatinous body oozing up and over his face on impact. The other boys watched with amusement as Toni clawed at the mass, trying desperately to dislodge it. Moogie slime was sticky, and getting one to let go required either a close explosion or fire.

Jessup used his second primer before the boy ran out of air or fell into a clam nest.

"Christ!" Toni shouted, and Loko intercepted a third moogie, aiming for Toni's legs with a net. The creature's meat was only edible if they were caught live and smoked. Blast shock made everything bitter and funky.

The creatures normally slept during the day, but the nearly transparent things became invisible in the dusk and dark. Night fishing, when other things came out of the forest, was too dangerous, so tossing a blasting cap in to wake them up and then having someone stand on the bank and wave their arms around and shout as bait was a good afternoon sport.

Jessup watched a large moogie surface then suck back down and jet out of the water, headed straight for Loko and Alec as they worked to get the first net clear and onto the drying rack beside their small fire. He ran forward, thinking to shout, and put his net out as a spear, catching the creature, and watched it travel up the spear and fly straight into his face.

He could see. He knew the creature's only weapon was to engulf and suffocate, so he held his breath and watched through the wavy blur as Alec turned, saw the impact, stepped away, and then stepped forward, picking up a brand from the fire and moving quickly to force the moogie off of Jessup's face. The creature retracted grudgingly, and it was several suffocating minutes of clinging to his net pole and refusing to exhale before his face was clear and he sank to his knees. He smelled of burnt moogie and laughed as Alec offered him a hand to stand.

"We should move back a bit. These guys are dicks," Alec said solemnly, and Jessup nodded with a grin.

#

The sun dropped behind the tree wall and Sheila put down her spinning. She needed a bath, she decided, and moved about the cabin, straightening things up.

Her C&C chimed and she picked it up to see Patty's face and the number twenty-two.

"I can't be what you need," she said to the communication computer and set it back down, unanswered.

Her small cabin had a sit bath and shower behind the rocket stove and she drew scalding water into it before adding cold water until it was comfortable to her hand.

Dropping her pants and shirt on the floor beside the tall tub, she stepped into the water and knelt to sit on the ledge. The water was hot, and she wished she had thought to add a bit of scented oil as she soaked and slowly used a pumice stone to cut back on the calluses.

The water was cloudy and cooling off when she decided to stop sanding away at her left foot. Fingernails, toenails, elbows, heels, knees, and lately the bottom edge of her lower lip, all grew coarse and crusty if she didn't scrub often and oil nightly.

She stepped out of the tub, wrapped a towel about her, picked up her clothes and walked through the dark cabin to her room. Sitting on her bed, she dropped her clothes and towel onto the floor, and poured a small amount of mint-scented oil into her hand, and rubbed her left foot, paying special care to her nailbeds and heel.

The nightly routine was soothing. It was something that Ryan always left during, he said to give her privacy, but she saw the way he would look at her random stone scabs when he thought she couldn't see. She knew that he preferred to wait until she was oiled and soft before coming to bed, that he preferred them to sleep in their pajamas and her in socks so there was no chance of her scratching him in the night.

Tonight, she oiled her body and then slid under the covers, her hand still gently sliding around her body, reintroducing her to herself, as she waited for sleep and her dream lover to return.

#

"Answer, answer, answer," Patty said impatiently as she thumbed off the call without leaving a message and called the next number in her queue.

"Answer, answer, please answer," she said again, pacing her kitchen in the near dark, and gulping alcohol-laced too-hot tea. She thumbed off the second call and tried a third number for the first time.

"This is Jessup Tranger," the voice said loudly. Patty froze and checked the screen to see if it was his message line. "You there, Mrs. Pries?"

"Oh, Chief, thank the Spirits," Patty exclaimed and for a moment the fear eased.

"What's wrong?" Chief Tranger asked, his voice full of concern.

"I can't get my husband Jeff on the C&C," she answered and then blurted out, "We talk every night, and he never misses a call. Not even when the slide killed my brother Ryan. He always calls me at bed time. Always," she finished and the fear and tears threatened to overwhelm her.

"Now, Mrs. Pries, you know communications with the outer camps can be tricky. They've missed check-ins before, but if it makes you feel any better, I will send someone out tomorrow if he hasn't called by nine am. OK?" The chief offered more than she expected and Patty nodded through her tears before gulping and agreeing.

"Ok, please call me in the morning when he calls," Tranger said and Patty heard the line disconnect.

#

Ell Menedez tried to call Chief Tranger first, but his line went straight to message and she told him to call Waits when he got the message.

Her second call caught Beth in the middle of a call with Haily Peters about missing chickens.

"Hey, Ell," Beth said, and Ell thought the other woman sounded happy to hear from her. They weren't friends. Beth's brusque personality and habit of playing stickball better than most guys instead of hanging out with the girls in her class had never given them reason to be friends.

"Sheriff," Ell said quickly, needing the other woman to understand that it was important and not a social call.

"Ms. Menedez?" Beth replied, and Ell felt relief at that simple change in tone. She didn't take time to think about it anymore than Martin Cosery thought about why he approached the one teacher every kid hated simply because he was also the one teacher with a gun.

"Martin Cosery came to school at noon without his brother, he looked tired, and after school he asked Jacob Waits to walk him home. His mother never came for him and he looked like hell," Ell explained.

"He's six?" Beth asked.

"Eight, brother is six. They live opposite the stickball field, against the raspberry field." Ell finished as a wisp of cold air caressed her cheek. "Hold on," she whispered.

And her first husband drifted into the classroom to stand in front of her.

"The skinwalker is running," the spirit said. "Burn sage, burn grass, burn the fields. They are awake." And the ghost faded into dust.

"I heard," Beth said in a soft voice when Ell didn't speak for a minute.

"Jacob took Martin to his place, and I left a message for the chief," Beth said and lit a single sage leaf to smolder. "Be careful," she added but Beth had disconnected.

#

"Would you like a few raspberries?" Jacob offered the boy and saw a look of terror flash through the kid's eyes before the shell-shock returned. "Or hazelnut butter?"

"Yes, sir," Martin said in a whisper, and Jacob put a bowl of crackers on the table with a small jar of hazelnut butter.

"Do you drink tea or coffee?" Jacob asked and then shook his head, reminding himself of the boy's age.

"Coffee, sir. Mama said it slows me down," Martin whispered.

"Indeed, let me put some water on." Jacob moved to the stove and checked to see if there was water in his kettle. The idea that the child's mother would try to medicate his behavior problems with caffeine didn't surprise him and he made a note to himself to talk to Westover about options tomorrow.

"I don't know that you need slowed down tonight. How do you feel?" he asked the boy as he mixed up the toasted grains and bitter Felist herb to brew a pot of the vile mix that everyone swore he would develop a taste for eventually. The lavender flavored tea was at least smooth.

"I drank a lot last night, sir. I feel slow," Martin said, and Jacob realized that the boy hadn't helped himself to the food in front of him.

"Eat something," Jacob encouraged as the water started to steam. "Your mom let you drink coffee last night?" he probed.

"My gramma came and told me to, 'cause mom was outside," Martin answered in a flat voice and took a bite of a dry cracker.

"Here," Jacob said and slathered some creamy hazelnut butter onto a new cracker for the boy. The child accepted the cracker and stared at it for a long time.

Jacob turned away and poured off the brewed coffee into a new pot before returning to the table and pouring two mugs. He pulled the bowl of sweet lime toward himself and scooped two large spoonfuls into each cup before moving to his icebox and getting a quart of cream. He used the sugar spoon to hold the risen cream to the side of the wide-mouthed crock, and poured cream into each cup as well.

"Tommy is hungry too," the boy said. "Gramma is with him," he added as he put the cracker into his mouth carefully and then reached out to accept his coffee.

"I've never met your grandmother," Jacob said and took a long drink of his coffee. He knew what the boy was about to say and he didn't want his annoyance to ruin his appetite.

"She died," the boy said, and Jacob worked to not frown. "I think my mom died," he added, and Jacob choked on his coffee.

It was what he was afraid of, but to have an eight-year-old say it so calmly shook him to the core.

"She went to pick raspberries and then Ms. Evans was screaming and Mr. Evans was crying and Gramma said to close the door and get Tommy food," the boy finished, staring off into space, and Jacob turned to look at the wall.

"Is she here now?" he asked.

"No, she's with Tommy. Can I live with you?" Martin asked and turned tear-filled eyes to break Jacob's heart.

"You can stay with me as long as you need to. Let's get you ready for bed," Jacob said and realized that he meant it.

#

Someone's screaming.

Westover sat up in bed and reached down for his pants.

Chapter 9

Projected Earth date: 2132

Planet Date: 0105, Mid-Warm

Coyote's Winter House, Rex Tyrol, Designated Choctaw Emigration planet, Kanto Corporation

Dr. William Westover never planned to be a small colony doctor. He never planned to be a small colony anything. He was born in Tokyo and relocated to New Jersey in his teens. His mom took a Fujin Corp job right about the time he discovered girls, and he became a medical research veterinarian's assistant for the pharmaceutical company that held seven of the two hundred and ninety-three patents necessary for the basic Pro-gen treatments. It was a simple, low-stress job at Pranumic, with decent pay and plenty of pretty red-headed secretaries to choose from while learning the company secrets.

He also wasn't named William Westover back then. That name was picked from a reader board while waiting for the Fujin agent to make the deal that would see him set financially.

Only a two-bit civil terrorist sprayed the train platform with Moler-Gen while he was waiting. A nasty piece of nano-war tech that attacked his DNA. Fujin never retrieved the data, never paid the promised cash, and the Feds investigating the train attack were happy enough to have the stolen files that they let him go for Pro-gen before the damage was too extensive.

William Westover left progressive genetic therapy four years later with a rating for cellular kinetics. He could visualize and move small things with his mind. He turned down the first dozen job offers and took a US Navy contract. Halfway through vet tech training, he scored a bit too high on something and found himself in the surgical sub-intern program, working with humans not animals. A couple of disciplinary actions later and he was simply a Corpsman and on a ship full of Marines.

Dr. Westover hated the small colony, dreamed of big city lights and dance floor conquests, but mostly he hated the home-brew beer and paint-thinner shine that wasn't enough. It was never enough.

Someone's screaming.

He froze, one leg in his pants as the image of a woman's naked body, sprawled across a path, half in

the silver grass and covered in a thousand razor-clean
cuts, came to him. The image shifted from the woman
just as Westover realized that one of her legs was
missing at the mid-thigh in a fairly clean amputation
line, to be replace by Patty, who was staring him
straight in the eye and screaming. Her face contorted in
horror, her red hair tangled, makeup smeared. Westover
blinked and forced the hot-link image back.

He finished getting dressed in a hurry and
jogged the path toward the power station.

#

"Did anyone touch the body?" Tranger was
asking as Westover arrived, out of breath.

No one spoke from the small crowd and
Westover didn't see or hear Patty in the group.

"Why would she run through the silver grass?"
someone asked.

Crawled, Westover used a foot to flip the body
over and confirm that her arms were torn to ribbons,
bare bone on the palms of her hands and remaining
knee.

Need to see the bone, a voice said over the
crowd.

"I know my job," Westover said in annoyance
and then pulled rubber-lined metal mesh gloves from

his bag to handle the body without worrying about the silver grass poison that was in every cut and scratch.

"I know you do, Doc," Tranger said and moved between the doctor and the crowd. "Let's give him room folks."

"Shelly Cosery." The name was murmured from one person to the next as Westover placed one hand on the woman's hip and leaned out over the body in a plank to finally get a glimpse of the end of the amputated leg bone.

Bugs.

Buy some time.

They can panic tomorrow.

"Chief," he said loudly, moving away from the body and standing up. "Chief," he said again, quieter, and that got everyone's attention. "She lost the leg to the rot. Must have been insanely painful, drove her into the grass," he lied and saw Jessup Tranger squint to study him.

But the crowd seemed to accept it and people moved away in the moonlight.

"The body isn't safe to handle," he continued, holding eye-contact as he fastidiously peeled his gloves off and placed them in a red metal box.

"We'll get some rope and some canvas, and move her to the cemetery," Tranger said.

"Won't work. Not worth the risk," Westover said bluntly, and turned away, staring down at the body and ignoring Tranger's frown.

"The silver grass poison is drying already. It'll be dust and airborne soon. Not a good risk for anyone," he explained.

And the silver grass was a good excuse. The razor sharp blades were wet with a cyanide-based poison that, when separated from the plant, dried into lethal powder that floated when disturbed and was known to work its way through simple masks. It broke down with sunlight or heat and would be rendered harmless soon enough. The poison was pretty obvious in a victim and murder cases were fairly uncommon. Accidents and stupidity happened at a higher rate, and everyone on the colony had a healthy fear of the grass and its poison.

"Are you suggesting we try to hose her down first?" Tranger asked.

Fire.

"Fire," Westover offered and walked away, looking for Patty.

#

"Jacob?" the soft voice echoed from outside, and Jacob Waits blinked against the moonlight streaming in his living room window. Martin Cosery was fast asleep on his couch and Jacob had dozed off reading while waiting for Beth Pyle to get back to him about the boy's mom.

"Jacob," Patty's voice, he realized, whispered from his front door, accompanied by a faint knock.

He sighed and stood to answer the door for the colony's paranoid alcoholic.

"Shhh," he said in an exaggerated whisper and then stepped outside to talk to her.

She was in the same bathrobe as the morning, one slipper was missing, and her hair was falling out of its braid, but the first thing he noticed was how beautiful she was, even with her red and swollen eyes shining in the bright light of the false dawn.

"Jeff didn't call me tonight and she's dead," Patty blurted out and tears overwhelmed her.

Jacob found himself holding the sobbing woman as her body shook and she struggled for air.

"You're safe," he said and wondered if this was a real crisis or another of Patty's panics. "You're safe," he repeated.

"Jeff's dead," she sobbed. Only it wasn't the first time she convinced herself that her husband was dead and it wasn't the first time she ran to Jacob for sympathy. The first time had been an emotional night as he believed her and was relieved in the following days to find out that she was sterile and seemed to have forgotten.

"Now, Patty, why do you think Jeff's dead?" he asked.

"He never called me," she said and wiped her nose with her sleeve.

"He's missed a call or two before. Wait. Who's dead?" Jacob asked as the other comment registered.

"I saw a skinwalker," Patty replied, all red eyes and breathless voice and Jacob realized that she was trying to seduce him.

"A spirit?" he asked and felt his patience fading as the woman moved to tighten the belt on her house coat but succeeded in opening the neckline.

'No, a skinwalker. He killed her." Patty reached into her housecoat pocket and pulled a small bottle of alcohol out.

"Killed who?" Jacob asked impatiently, but Patty stopped mid-drink to stare in horror behind him.

Jacob turned slowly, trying to keep an eye on the hysterical, intoxicated woman and saw Martin Cosery standing in the doorway behind him, wearing a borrowed work shirt as a nightgown.

Patty lowered her bottle, opening and closing her mouth without a sound, and then spun and ran down the path, screaming.

Jacob sighed, realizing that the woman must have jumped to a very wrong conclusion and waved the boy back inside.

#

The smell of smoke woke Sheila with the second moon's false dawn.

She was alone.

Lying naked in bed, she ran her hand over her flat belly and tried to picture the child inside of her. Ryan always wanted a girl, said boys were a waste of time when women lived twice as long. Always talked about using the anonymous sperm bank that Westover established for those who were sterile.

This was a boy and she was alone and no one had come to her in the night.

Sheila felt the first few tears start, tried to push them back the way she had been doing in the weeks since Ryan's death. Tried to numb herself. Empty her emotions.

Only, it was a boy, the doctor confirmed the pregnancy, her mother named him, and Sheila couldn't block the facts.

Ryan was dead.

The tears fell as she sat up in bed slowly and then stood to dress like a robot. But she wasn't numb and the pain just kept rolling through in wave after wave of brutal reality.

Ryan was dead.

She was alone.

Pregnant.

Smoke.

And the tears were gone as she stood in her kitchen and smelled the grass fire.

There was a field fire when she was seven years old, and her father had a flashback to when the Marines came. He relived the night they burned everything to wipe out the bugs, and put cloth in the door jam and up the chimney. He said the cloth slowed the bugs, and he hid in the closet, listening for explosions, the fire outside, and talked about the sound of the bugs on the metal roof. He whispered about when his world was gray with ash and only the Marines remained, until her mother came home and coaxed him out of his fear.

He wasn't the only one affected, and for weeks the adults in her life shared stories and alcohol trying to forget.

Sheila stood, frozen, listening for bugs or Marines or explosions.

Patty's wailing was a shock.

"He killed her!" the other woman cried clearly as she ran past the cabin.

Sheila thought about making a cup of coffee, but moved to the door instead.

Patty was running from cabin to cabin, screaming the same declaration over and over again as she went. "He killed her!"

And Sheila wasn't the only person to step out and look around, confused.

The smell of the grass fire couldn't be ignored from outside and Sheila watched a group of neighbors moving toward the lookout tower.

Thumbing her C&C on, she called Dr. Westover.

"I'm busy," was the curt answer, but he didn't hang up.

"Patty just ran by my cabin screaming 'He killed her.' Should I be worried?" Sheila asked and returned to her kitchen to put water on to boil.

"Who is this?" Westover demanded and Sheila frowned that he hadn't read his screen before answering.

"Sheila," she replied.

"What direction?" he countered, and Sheila could hear him struggling to breathe.

"Toward the blue trail," she replied, waiting for more information but the line went dead.

She thumbed her unit to call Beth Pyle but it went straight to message as did Chief Tranger's. Pouring a cup of coffee, she stared out of her window and decided that "he" wasn't a bug or a skinwalker and locked her kitchen door, taking a moment to push a rug against the door jam, and retreated to her living room to sew.

#

Beth Pyle knew she was dead. The grub was chewing its way through the shed wall and it was just a matter of time before her and the boy, Tom Cosery, would be eaten. She shot nine grubs to get to the shed, only one remained and its sharp teeth had found a wooden corner of the shed where someone had repaired the mortar and stone with wood in the past. The grub was chewing louder than the boy's quiet sobs.

No one came to investigate the gunshots, and she realized that the bugs must have gotten into the nearby houses.

She had an empty gun, a small knife, and a can of hot spray for drunken idiots. None of which was helpful against a grub. Lone bugs came out of the forest from time to time, usually going for the first cow they encountered; this one got the Cosery's dog. Beth had come to check on the family at Jacob Waits' insistence.

She found the remains of the dog and a bunch of small grubs looking for a new meal. She would be dead already, but the boy came around the corner of the house, screaming, and threw a bucket of fireplace coals at the grubs, and then tried to run back inside.

Only the grubs were fast and they scattered and ran for him, and Beth spent her magazine buying the kid time to get to the shed when two grubs blocked his path to the house.

That was hours ago and she had lost her C&C someplace outside.

"This burns," the boy said, and Beth looked down to see him offering her a jerry can. She knelt beside him and opened the can to confirm that it contained fuel alcohol.

"My gamma said they don't like smelly stuff," and Beth knew without asking that he was talking about a spirit.

She nodded and took off her overshirt to tear it into strips. The boy waited patiently while she soaked two strips down with the fuel and pushed them against the board that was being attacked by the grub. She stood and felt her pockets for a lighter, and he tugged on her hand to offer one.

Beth smiled at the boy, even as the sound of the grub chewing grew louder and the smell of the fuel told her they would probably die from asphyxiation when she lit the rags. Better than the grubs, she decided.

"The skinwalker comes," a woman's voice said clearly, though only a whisper.

"Gamma," the boy called out, and the grub was silent as the shed door was kicked inward and light framed someone in the doorway.

\#

"Answer your damn phone!" Jacob said as Tranger's line went straight to message again, and he tried another number.

"Westover!" Jacob shouted when the doctor answered his phone. "Patty said someone was dead?"

"Where is she?" Westover demanded and Jacob frowned.

"What the hell happened? I sent the sheriff out to check on someone and now Patty is drunk and saying a skinwalker killed a woman. Tranger is nowhere to be found. So you tell me, what is going on?" he demanded and his anger was close to overwhelming him.

"I don't know about the sheriff. Shelly Cosery is dead. I don't know where the hell Patty is, and Chief Tranger is doing his job. Now get off my fucking line and make yourself useful," Westover snapped.

And Jacob made eye-contact with Martin Cosery. The boy didn't look surprised.

"Wait!" Jacob shouted before Westover could disconnect. "I sent Beth out to the Cosery place to check on them at around 5pm. Patty was running toward the Northwest lookout tower; she keeps a stash there," and he didn't explain how he knew that. "If Tranger will answer your calls, please tell him we need to talk."

"Done," Westover said, and the line went dead.

"Your mom," Jacob started to say and found he had no words for the boy. Martin moved to stand beside him and slipped a small hand into his own. Jacob looked away when the boy patted his arm reassuringly.

"Light some sage," a tired woman's voice echoed through the room, and Jacob wasn't surprised. He had never believed in the spirits because he had never seen or heard one, but now he knew they were real.

"Grandmother," he called out with respect. "Please help Martin's brother, Tom," Jacob asked the room in a near prayer.

A whisper of cold air and a whirl of dust was the answer.

"Let's get you dressed again," Jacob said to Martin as his C&C chimed with Tranger's call.

"What?" the hief demanded, and Jacob knew he hadn't listened to his messages.

"Ms. Cosery is dead?" Jacob asked.

"Yes, I'm busy," Tranger replied but didn't cut the call.

"I have Martin Cosery here with me. Beth went out to their place to check on the family before dusk," Jacob said and handed Martin a flannel shirt to wear as a coat.

"Fuck!" Tranger cursed and Jacob nodded.

"A spirit told me they don't like sage," Jacob said, and he and Martin moved to the front door.

"Who doesn't like sage?" Tranger demanded.

"Spirit didn't say, but I got the impression that it wasn't the skinwalker. Cosery was picking raspberries two nights ago, kid says the neighbors screamed and a spirit told him to close the door. The spirit said the younger boy is still out there alive," Jacob said and waited for Tranger to process as he and Martin started walking toward the school. The raspberry fields would be ahead on his left and he appreciated the fact that Martin had taken his right side, and walked just ahead of him and clear of his weapon.

"Talkative spirit," was all Tranger said.

"Long night," Jacob retorted, not feeling like explaining that the information came from several sources. "I'm heading for the school now," he added.

"Go to the power station. Tell Kim to light everything we got. If it's the bugs, we'll spend the power while we have it." Tranger said, and the line went dead.

#

"Gamma?" Tommy whispered, and Beth stared at the older man in confusion.

The light was behind him and haloed his short, nearly white hair as he pivoted and scanned the yard from the doorway.

"Come on," Beth said to Tommy, who ran to the back of the shed, almost out of her reach. The fuel can tipped over as she tried to reach the boy, and the fumes made her eyes water.

"Light the fire," whispered the old woman's voice, and Beth turned in time to see the man's surprise at the voice.

"Ok, Gamma," Tommy said and moved to stand beside Beth. "I think I left the kitchen door open," the boy added.

"Not safe," the man said in a voice so rough Beth suspected that it had been a long time since he had spoken. He stepped out of the shed door and Beth followed, digging in her pocket for the lighter Tommy had given her.

In the moon's first dawn she could see that the man was old, older than her mother even, and healthy. No sign of the rot. The smell of smoke drew her attention back into the shed and she saw six-year-old Tommy standing in a pool of spilled fuel, lighting the strips of her shirt that she had placed against the wood boards.

Before she could dart in to grab the boy, the man was past her, picked up the boy and the fuel can, and spun to retreat from the growing fire. He met her eyes as he approached, starting to hand the boy to her as a package when his eyes squinted to focus just behind and above her.

Beth ducked and brought her hands up on instinct, and the bug overshot her to land on the flat of the shed door, inches from the man, who smashed it in passing and joined her outside.

The shed fire grew and Beth's eyes followed the smoke up to see five or six large black bugs circling the area between the shed and the house.

"There were grubs," she said and reached out to take Tommy from the man.

Her gun was useless and his reflexes were better, and she hoped he had a plan as he moved away from the smoldering shed a few feet and watched the bugs circling. A few more feet from the fire and smoke and a bug dived for him. Beth started to suck in her breath and warn him but he shifted left, rolled right, and was on his feet and back beside her in a blur.

The Marines from her childhood moved like that. She remembered them fighting each other after the bugs, before they all wandered away. Her mother and father used to talk about them. Used to be afraid of them. Said they were all crazy from the Pro-gen that made them fast and strong. Said it was for the best when only Westover remained.

"You're a soldier," Beth said, and the glance he gave her made her feel stupid for wasting time and breath to state the obvious in a crisis.

"Marine," he corrected in his raw voice and poured out a handful of fuel and wet his hair and shoulders carefully with it. Then he moved away from the heat of the burning shed and waited for the bugs to notice him.

Beth held her breath and tried to settle Tommy onto her hip, but the boy wanted down. The Marine made it across the yard without a bug trying to kill him.

Beth poured some fuel into her own hand and patted it into Tommy's dirty hair. The boy watched the Marine as Beth poured more fuel and she saw the danger in the child's eyes before she heard the crack of a bug being hit by a stick above her head.

A second man came from the side of the shed, gave her a tight nod and stood over her as she soaked Tommy's shirt with the fuel before starting on her own hair and shirt.

"Run to the river," the spirit woman's voice said, and Beth watched the two men shift from looking toward the path that led through the raspberry field and to the school look at the side of the house where Beth first encountered the grubs.

"That's my Gamma," Tommy said loudly.

"Wise woman," the new man said in a voice barely a whisper.

One man picked up the almost empty fuel can and the second picked up Tommy, and with a quick glance to Beth, they moved around the house at a cautious jog.

#

Don't bother with the drunk.

She is trouble.

Westover stumbled on the path as the image of a kitchen full of grubs and body pieces, seen through a window, replaced the path for a moment.

She is dying.

She has nothing to lose.

She told Waits we killed the woman.

His vision was clouded by smoke from Tranger's fire and the sight of the chief yelling into his phone. Westover slowed his jog and glanced around to orientate himself as the brown moon started to glow.

Don't like her.

Don't trust her.

Don't bother.

The sight of a bug, sitting on a grounded flutterby, was replaced by the sight of Lonco smashing the bug with a rock before it could pull its ovipositor out and relaunch.

People will listen to her, waste time.

Fuck her.

She's sterile.

Trey's face glinted in the reflection of a window and Westover glimpsed Sheila sleeping on a couch.

Found the sheriff and kid.

Don't waste time on the drunk.

And Westover saw Lonco standing in the door of a garden shed, looking for threats, as he protected someone behind him.

Hysterics become accusations.

"Patty!" Westover called out as he approached the observation tower.

Hurry.

"Patty!" Westover shouted again from the base of the five-story tower. Stopping at the ladder, Westover closed his eyes and stilled his mind. He felt

the others push against the link and then fade, a
lingering resentment ghosted through the link as he
shifted his mind to feel for organic life above him.

A wall of screaming pain and emptiness hit him
and he slammed down his shields against Patty's
drunken hysterics, before allowing the hot-link to
reform. He was the only one who could block it at all,
and then only for seconds if he was using his Pro-gen
developed skills. The other minds flooded back into
him and for seconds he couldn't separate his senses
from the others.

Phillips' heart was stressed and he focused on
the pain until the other body slowed down and allowed
himself to rest.

"I'm coming up, Patty," Westover called out
and climbed the ladder.

\#

"Kim!" Jacob shouted into the door intercom.
He didn't have the code for the door memorized and
right now deep inside the shuttle seemed the safest
place he could take Martin.

"Kim!" he shouted again re-thumbing the door
call. The door buzzed and popped open an inch, and
Jacob Waits shoved his way into the airlock with the
boy right behind him. He didn't know what was
happening in the colony, but two fires were burning,
people weren't answering his calls, and a woman was
dead.

The cavernous cargo bay was dark and only the light of the control room door gave him courage to move forward.

Kim stood in the doorway, impatiently waiting.

Martin clung to his hand and then stared around the control room as they entered behind Kim.

"Halito, Waits, what do you want?" Kim asked.

And Jacob was taken aback by the swirls of dust that seemed to just be settling in the room.

"Lots of spirits," Martin whispered.

"What did they say?" Jacob asked, not answering Kim's rudeness.

"They said that if I torched the mainline and blew up the shuttle I could sit at the fire with them," Kim replied with a shrug as she moved to check dials. "You interrupted their sales pitch."

Jacob took a moment to process what she said. Tried to not think of the reason previous power stations were destroyed.

"I think the bugs are back," he finally said, and Kim turned to stare at him. He had only been on the planet for three years and she was twenty-one years old. Neither of them had more than other people's stories about what the bugs were or how bad it could be.

"Look," Martin said and broke the moment of locked eyes.

A swirl of dust coalesced into a flutterby and then shifted to a man in a Colonial Marine drop uniform, torn and bloody, his left hand ended at a bound stump. The spirit studied a screen, moved to a second, and seemed to be looking for something.

"The relief valve cut-off is over here," Kim said and the spirit turned to face them. The man was young, his eyes shone with fear and determination, he opened his mouth to speak just as Jacob's phone chimed.

And the spirit was gone.

"We need the fucking lights!" Tranger shouted over the line and cut the call before Jacob could respond.

"Shit," Kim said and moved to work the consoles.

"Timing," Jacob agreed as the shuttle started to hum from the power. "Light up every line, make it daylight out there," he added and watched the young woman work carefully.

#

"Patty," Westover said when he cleared the platform and turned to see the woman curled up on a bench, crying in deep, heart-wrenching sobs.

"Here," he said and moved to sit beside her, to hold her as she cried. It was several long minutes before she struggled to control her sobbing and a few more before she blew her nose on the sleeve of her filthy bathrobe and then snuggled into his side inappropriately.

It wasn't the first time she decided to seduce him, and Westover patiently removed her hand from his crotch as he shifted away on the bench.

"Are you okay?" he asked her, without much hope. He just wanted to know where her brain was tonight.

"I saw a skinwalker," she whispered. "He killed her," she said in a serious tone, through hiccups and an alcohol-induced slur.

"You don't want people to know you were drinking," Westover said quietly, hoping to deflect her.

"He killed her," Patty insisted and twisted her hands together.

"Here," Westover said, and offered her a small flask from his own pocket.

"I saw him," she insisted and Westover watched her down the contents of the flask in a single swallow. "Jacob took the boy," she added as she slid toward unconsciousness.

Westover stood to look down at the woman as she slumped on the bench.

"Leave us alone," a man's voice said, and Westover looked sideways at the spirit forming in dust beside him.

"It'll take an hour," Westover said about the overdose in the flask he gave Patty to drink, as he reached out to smooth her hair.

"Leave us alone," the spirit repeated and moved to sit on the bench with his daughter.

#

The shuttle spire flashed a white strobe that quickly became a beacon light that lit up the colony from the hunter tree wall to the rivers, and for the first time that night, Chief Jessup Tranger was afraid.

Directly in front of him, he could clearly see two bugs laying eggs on a downed flutterby, and he had no weapon.

A blasting cap detonated between the two bugs, and though not dead, neither was able to fly.

Alec shot him a grin and the two continued across on the path through the raspberries toward the Cosery house.

The first cluster of houses against the field was quiet, doors were open, and Jessup wondered how they could have lost people so close to the school without warning calls or alarms being sounded.

"Must have been fast," Alec commented as they saw a fire bloom in the next cluster of houses less than half a mile away. They took off running toward the fire and Jessup knew it was a bad idea.

With the light of the shuttle spire out-shining first dawn, people moved about inside some of the houses they passed. Completely unaware of the carnage that Jessup glimpsed in corners of yards and through windows.

Jessup's C&C chimed, then Alec's, and they stopped to answer them.

"This is Assistant Chief Waits. Stay in your home. There is nothing to worry about. Stay in your home and wait for the all clear," came over the speakers and Jessup frowned before thumbing off his C&C and continuing toward the fire.

Walking between two houses, Alec behind him, Jessup spun in time to see Alec vomit uncontrollably and then straighten to meet his eyes. The kid was pale and shook up, and Jessup regretted letting him come along to check on Beth.

Alec pointed in the window of the house beside them to the North and Jessup moved to look in. A ribcage on the floor beside a stuffed animal, sausages on the table, and two bloated, unmoving grubs by the closed door. Only the sausages had fingernails and the stuffed animal was the skin of a headless dog, and Jessup's mind shifted to see the carnage in the room.

"Let's go," was all he said, regretting the decision to go into the narrow alley.

Approaching the fire, Jessup saw a dog skeleton in the yard and dead grubs, their bright colors easy to spot on the path. The bullet holes were just as easy to see.

The garden shed was smoldering, door open, roof gone and Jessup moved into the ruin, carefully looking for bones.

"She's not here," Alec said, and Jessup nodded.

"Let's get back to the shuttle," Jessup said. Dawn had come without him noticing and people would want answers.

Chapter 10

Projected Earth date: 2132

Planet Date: 0105, Mid-Warm

Coyote's Winter House, Rex Tyrol, Designated Choctaw Emigration planet, Kanto Corporation

"Patty said Waits killed her!" someone shouted and Jacob Waits just shook his head in disbelief.

It was seven am and half of the colony seemed to have disregarded the order to stay inside and now gathered on the school stickball field, waiting for Chief Tranger and Assistant Chief Waits to make an announcement.

Tranger was thumbing and re-thumbing his C&C, trying to raise Sheriff Beth Pyle, while Waits listened to the crowd as it edged toward becoming a mob.

"Patty's a drunk," Westover said loudly and the pronouncement of the doctor gave validity to the rumor that was never quite addressed in the community.

Waits sighed with relief as the crowd quieted, thinking they had listened to Westover.

Beth Pyle walked from the back of the crowd to the front as people turned to stare. She carried a dirty and angry looking six-year-old Tom Cosery and, for a moment, Jacob had a worry that he was about to be lynched. Three gray-haired men followed her through the silent crowd and Waits had a moment of elation that forty wasn't the maximum lifespan for men on this godforsaken rock. He knew the rot was an exaggeration of the colonists.

Martin pushed past him, and Beth set Tom down.

"Your brother saved my life," she told Martin and then stood to almost fall into Chief Tranger's arms with a long-suppressed sob.

"I don't believe we've met," Jacob said and stepped forward to offer a handshake to the dark-skinned man closest to him.

Two of the men turned away from him together, and walked back through the crowd until they cleared the field, and then they broke into a jog and were gone around the corner of the power station.

The crowd was silent and still and Waits looked around to see fear on the older colonist's faces.

The third man was old, a black face with short white hair, and Jacob guessed his age at around late sixties to early seventies. He had deep wrinkles, threadbare clothes and newer boots that looked suspiciously like the pair Bill Peters raised a stink about being missing during Waits' first month in the colony, three years ago.

The man held his head high and moved to stand beside Westover, and Jacob realized that he and the other men were the Colonial Marines that people still talked about, twenty-six years after the bug incursion and seven years since the last one went crazy and walked into the hunter tree forest.

Westover frowned at him, and Waits realized that he was staring and looked down to see Martin and Tommy silently watching the Marine as well.

He turned away from Westover and company and knelt beside Martin to look closer at Tommy.

"You ok?" he asked and made eye-contact with the younger boy.

"Sheriff Beth shot the bugs and Gamma brought him to save us. They don't like fuel." The boy blurted out in a near shout, and the silence of the crowd behind him reminded Jacob that people were listening.

"Sheriff Beth is very brave," Waits said just as loudly as Tommy, with a nod, not breaking eye-contact and deciding right then to treat the two boys as closer to adults than children. "Your gramma told Martin and I that the bugs don't like sage or smoke," he added. "I'm glad the skinwalker saved you," Jacob finished and heard several people suck in their breath or outright gasp as they realized that the skinwalker that the spirits had been announcing was one of the Marines.

Jacob reached out and squeezed Tommy's shoulder in comfort, the same way he would have an adult, and then stood and faced the older man.

"Thank you for saving my friends," he said, and again offered his hand.

The older Marine continued to stare straight ahead for nearly a minute before turning his gaze toward Jacob and accepting the handshake.

Jacob noticed that the other man never quite made eye-contact and braced himself for a painful squeeze, but the hand shake was dry, moderate, and quick, and then the man was scanning the back of the crowd and the tree line three miles away.

"It's been a long night," Westover said, "come on," and he for waved the Marine to follow him through the crowd.

"Wait!" Chief Tranger said as he released Beth from his side and stepped toward Westover and the Marine. Something in the glance both men shot him froze Tranger for a moment.

"Are the bugs returning?" was shouted from the crowd.

"What do we do?"

"Did Waits kill the woman?" a third voice questioned, and Jacob clenched his jaw to keep from calling out an insult.

The Marine stopped and turned back while Westover kept walking away.

"There is a small hive in the raspberry field. Light smudge fires around the colony and flood the field, they should swarm and leave at dusk. Everyone lock up for a few nights and listen to your elders," the man said calmly in a hoarse near-whisper before turning and following Westover.

The crowd was silent as the information registered.

"I need volunteers for smudge fires," Chief Tranger rattled off assignments as he moved through the crowd. "Beth, deputize some folks and go knock on every door from Eastline to the trees. Waits, organize sleeping space for folks in the school if they aren't certain they can secure their own houses. Alec, I need a dozen people for cleanup and burial; please pick people you think can handle it. Ell, I need every ancestor or spirit message written down; please start a logbook and have people recount what they've been told. We need to listen."

"Billy, please help Alec, it's bad. Miss Evers, I need a head count on the colony. Could you please use the voter logs and call each household and confirm their location and make sure they know to stay indoors for the next few nights?"

Jacob nodded in agreement.

"Tammy, we need the animals in the barns and locked up tight. Grab who you need and soak down a bunch of hay for smudges."

Jacob moved to stand beside Martin and Tommy again.

"Martin, you're in charge of a snack kitchen. Take your brother and go to the school kitchen, we won't have time for meals so I want you to fill every carry bottle with water and syrup, keep the cream jars and sweet lime bowls full, and find all the cookies and crackers in the kitchen and have them on the cafeteria tables so that people can come in, eat and drink, and leave; got it?"

Jacob pushed down a huge smile as the kid stood up straight and nodded solemnly at Tranger.

For the first time since emigrating, Jacob Waits saw the leadership mantle resting on Tranger's shoulders, and he wore it well.

#

She's safe.

Need to blow that power station.

Cause it worked so well the last time.

Need a radar ping to confirm.

That'll freak the civvies.

Need the shuttle to access the satellite.

It can wait.

Westover paused to close Patty's open gate before he and Phillips continued on to Sheila's house.

Chapter 11

Projected Earth date: 2132

Planet Date: 0105, Mid-Warm

Coyote's Winter House, Rex Tyrol, Designated
Choctaw Emigration planet, Kanto Corporation

"Why did they leave?" Ell asked Beth as they
moved past the school.

"They went crazy," Pete said from behind them
and the two women slowed to let Pete Baton catch up.
He was forty-two; he'd been seventeen years old when
the bugs hatched last, and now the rot forced him to use
a cane to walk.

"How? Why?" Beth and Ell asked at the same
time and Beth smiled at the other woman.

"They're all Pro-gen," Pete replied, and stopped to answer his C&C with a wave for them to continue without him.

"We can't break the hot-link, makes it hard to think," a man said as he stepped from the doorway of a passing house to walk beside Beth.

He wasn't one of the two who rescued her and the boy, and Beth tried to watch him from the corner of her eye while Ell stumbled on the level path twice for openly gawking. He was old, brown hair streaked through with gray turning white at the sides, squint wrinkles at his eyes, and he walked confidently without turning to look at her.

"Beth, Ell," Beth said and waved to include the other woman.

The man walked for several steps before replying and Beth suspected that he had to remember his own name.

"Metzger," he finally said.

"How many?" Beth asked.

"Five, maybe seven, and the Doc," was the answer.

"He never mentioned survivors," Beth said.

"Doubt you ever asked," he replied.

"Are we in trouble?" Ell interrupted.

"Do you want to be?" the man responded with a deliberate glance at the hint of cleavage Ell's blouse allowed, and Beth smirked as the other woman opened her mouth to respond, and then blushed, spun away, and hurried ahead on the path.

"Nice walk," the man commented in a loud voice and Beth allowed a quiet chuckle to escape.

"The bugs?" Beth prompted as they walked past the school toward her office. Half of her mind on getting more ammo for her pistol and retrieving her shotgun, Beth came to a complete stop as she processed the fact that an unarmed Colonial Marine was walking with her toward the colony's small armory. And she started walking again when he met her stare with a bland glance before rescanning the roofline and horizon.

"Intel was pretty certain it's a twenty-seven year cycle. Doc says it's only been twenty-six." His answer felt wrong to Beth, like he was reciting someone else's argument.

"What do you think?" she asked.

"I don't," was his reply as he stepped to the side of her office door and put his back to the wall as if on sentry duty.

Pete and Jeff Wimmers were waiting a few feet up the path and moved to join her by the unopened door.

"Chief says you're deputizing folk. We're here for ammo," Pete said, and tried to push past her to the door.

"I will be deputizing a few people from the volunteer roster, Pete. Don't remember seeing you at drills," she replied, and put her back against the door without opening it.

"Ah, Bethy, you know we're good to help," Jeff insisted in a whine, and Beth worked at not frowning as she deliberately stepped toward the two men. She could see several other people gathering up the path, watching.

"You can volunteer for the smudge fires. The barns will need help. Or you can go home. If you stay here, I will arrest you. Of course, the jail will be nice and safe tonight," and she made it sound like a mocking offer.

"Bitch," was Pete's only response as he stared at the Marine behind her and then slapped his brother's arm and walked away.

"Do you think the cafeteria needs help?" Jeff asked in a half-whisper, and Beth nodded with a sincere smile of encouragement.

"Hey, Sheriff," Wayne Tranger said as Jeff left in the opposite direction of his brother.

"Hey, Deputy," Beth answered and turned to enter the door code for her office. Wayne was Jessup's younger cousin and the two men looked like brothers.

"What do you need, boss?" Wayne asked from the doorway, and Beth realized that he was blocking the door deliberately even though the Marine, Metzger, hadn't tried to follow her inside.

"I'm going to give the Colonial Marines the inventory and codes," she said. "Get on the line and call up ten guys. We need to run fast, knock on doors, and mark houses for the burial crews," she added, refusing to acknowledge Wayne's look of concern as Metzger followed him into the small office.

"Burn the houses that have grubs," the Marine said and stood just inside the room, studying everything in short, tight glances.

"Oh," Beth said as she thought about his comment. "Yeah. We need ten to twenty people, it's going to be a long day, and we'll need fuel and runners," she finished as she unlocked the back office wall to pull the divider open and show the two-cell jail and walk-in safe at the back.

Beth took a black grease pen and wrote the door code, not the master code but the simple open code, on the door itself before opening the safe. If anything happened to the colony administration team, the safe would be accessible and her brother wouldn't be forced into a role she knew he didn't want.

Wayne and Metzger stared at the code for a moment, and when the door opened, Beth was almost embarrassed by the term armory.

Seven shotguns, two ancient bolt-action rifles, five handguns that landed with the Marines twenty-six years ago, twenty electric press-guns missing batteries that hadn't been serviced in her lifetime, and three incendiary rifles with four chemical drums between them.

The rest of the safe was taken up by cases and crates of ammunition. Calibers and specs were stamped on boxes that occasionally lined up with a weapon nearby. It was the result of confiscating ammunition from colonist's supplies without taking the weapon that was imported with it. Anyone could request an allotment of ammo for hunting or protection. And after they filled out all of the paperwork concerning what happened to the last allotment; they would be given a ration and reminded that discharging a weapon inside the colony valley pissed off the hunter trees and made everyone's life difficult for weeks.

With drone ships landing five hundred colonists every five years, and few things on the planet worth shooting at, there was a lot of ammunition.

"Do you have an inventory of who has what personal weapon?" Metzger asked as he rustled through a box of mixed rounds, pulling out one caliber to pocket and shoving the unwanted rounds to the side.

"Somewhere," Beth said. "Giving everyone ammo would get a lot of people shot in the dark. We aren't soldiers," she said, and he paused to look in her direction without making eye contact.

"Understood. We want their guns," he said and continued to dig for ammo.

"Never happen," Wayne said. "People have six to ten rounds, they would fight to keep their guns. Especially the newer immigrants."

Metzger stared off into space for a moment and then nodded.

"Who is staying to guard this?" the Marine asked as he finally moved from the ammo to pick up a shotgun and check its balance.

"Wayne," Beth said, "and two deputies."

The Marine nodded approval and moved toward the office entrance. "Let's go."

#

Westover knocked on Sheila's front door. Trey was still watching her house, and Phillips stepped to the side of the house and disappeared.

"I'm staying inside," Sheila said as she answered the door.

"Can I come in?" Westover asked.

She turned and waved him inside with barely a curious glance at the outside world. The smell of smoke still hung in the air and people could be heard shouting with urgency as the door closed behind him. Westover didn't understand why the Marines fixated on the grieving widow, didn't know how they had noticed her. He was just glad it happened and that Trey followed her from their camp and had brought the others in from the wild.

He could feel the hot-link, forward in his consciousness, stronger than it had been in years as they used his eyes to stare at her and flared his nose to catch her perfume in the air.

"There was a bug hatching last night," Westover told her as they moved into her kitchen and she prepared coffee without asking.

She paused with the hot water pot over the coffee pot, poured slowly, and then set it down on the counter.

"I'll change clothes and go help at the school; who's in charge there?" she asked as she picked the coffee pot up, poured Westover a cup, and then turned to put the pot back on the stove without pouring a cup for herself.

"You're safer here," Westover said, not drinking the hot coffee, but cradling his hand around the cup and staring at the steam. The hot-link distracted him with concern and desire mingled in a confused, impotent anger.

"There was something on my roof last night. Mother said they got in last time; my back window doesn't stay latched," she said in a flat voice.

Westover felt emotion from her bleed into the hot-link and, as he focused on her muted fear and grief, he realized that she was a natural empath. He reached a hand out to comfort her and from the moment he touched her arm, the hot-link faded to a dull hiss in the back of his mind. He could still feel it and, if he concentrated, he was sure he would be able to use it, but for a moment the whirl of thoughts and images was ignorable.

Then Sheila moved away from him and he was alone in the kitchen with the telepathic hot-link flooded with jealousy.

Walk away.

Who's her father? Westover thought.

Fuck you!

Westover concentrated to force his concern to the fore, *Lonco is shooting bad DNA, someone else is spawning empaths,* he insisted.

We could have more empaths in the third generation, I need to check my records, Westover forced through, and felt the others calm for a moment.

Not a priority.

After the bugs.

"Dr. Westover," Sheila called from the next room and he moved from the kitchen to find her standing in the doorway from her bedroom to the main room holding a double-barreled shotgun and a shoulder sack heavy with what he suspected was ammunition. "Do you need this or should I take it to the school?"

Take it!

"I'm sure they have weapons at the school, thank you," he said and accepted the weapon quickly. Shouldering the shotgun and then the bag, without checking its contents. He still had his sidearm at his cabin, along with several other confiscated weapons and a decent stockpile of ammo gathered over the years.

"I'm ready," she said and walked to the front door without looking back.

Opening the door revealed a spirit, all dust and sunbeams, as if it had been waiting.

"Jacob RunsLightly."

Westover and Sheila waited as the spirit hung in the doorway.

We need better intel.

Ask if there are bugs near the station.

Is this the main hatch?

Westover shook his head at the mental shouts and wanted to reach out to take Sheila's hand now that he knew she could offer relief.

"They do not tell heat from clean fire. Light and smoke and water drive them away. Your friends do not sit by the fire. You cannot learn in the dark. Talk to us," and the spirit was gone.

Shit! someone said, and then the Marines went silent as they considered the info.

Chapter 12

Projected Earth date: 2132

Planet Date: 0105, Mid-Warm

Coyote's Winter House, Rex Tyrol, Designated Choctaw Emigration planet, Kanto Corporation

"Put that on the red table," the older Cosery boy said and pointed toward the table closest to the main cafeteria door.

Sheila stood just inside the door and watched the eight-year-old boy direct several older kids and Jeff Wimmer in setting out prepared foods and cups.

"Hi," Tommy Cosery said as he walked past her carrying a large bowl full of shriveled, stale frybread. His small arms wrapped around the bowl that tipped toward his face.

Sheila reached out and took the bowl before any frybread fell to the floor.

"Hi," she said with a smile to the boy Westover told her was an orphan now.

"Over there," Tommy said, pointing at the table against the window line and then walked away.

Sheila sat the bowl on the table, moved a few pieces around, and then stared out the window as Marc Jacobs and Tom Pyle ran by with shotguns slung across their backs and fuel cans in each hand.

The early noon sun was almost to the ridgeline and Sheila frowned as she stared at the trees that glowed silver blue.

"We need to close the shutters," she called out to anyone listening and then tried to crank the metal shutter closed on the window in front of her. The gears hadn't been oiled and she doubted that the shutters had been closed since they were installed when the school was built twenty-four years ago. The metal whined and screamed and then stopped only halfway closed.

Sheila moved to the next shutter.

"Mr. Waits will fix it when he comes," Martin Cosery said to her as she succeeded in almost closing the second shutter. Sheila turned her attention to the boy.

"I'll close the ones I can, and the shutters and vents in the kitchen, then I'll find some oil and try to fix them myself. No reason to worry Mr. Waits if we can do it ourselves." She didn't add that she thought the assistant chief wasn't worth a bucket of warm spit at a house fire, as her mother had said to the man's face during the last election.

"Chief Tranger said I was in charge of the cafeteria," the boy said and Sheila looked down to see him watching the other kids work. He was trembling and sad and Sheila watched him take a deep breath and make a decision. "You work on the shutters and vents. Let me know if you need anything," he said meeting her gaze and then walked away before she could smile.

The four shutters in the front of the cafeteria refused to shut completely, and Sheila moved from the last stuck shutter toward the kitchen when she felt someone watching her. She paused, looked around, and spotted the swirl of dust and air as the spirit coalesced in front of Jeff Wimmer.

"A man turned to hate is a rabid dog to be shot," the spirit said clearly.

"I don't have a gun," Jeff mumbled, and Sheila watched the man bow his head and drag his foot in an uncomfortable circle as if he was being lectured by an angry parent.

"Coward," the spirit said in a soft hiss and was gone.

Sheila watched Jeff Wimmer stand, downcast and unmoving, until Tommy Cosery walked up to him and slid a small hand into his and led him toward the kitchen.

"Shutters need oil," a hoarse male voice said behind her, and Sheila turned to see one of the Marines standing in the cafeteria doorway.

He was tall, his sunburnt face showcased honey-brown eyes and light brown hair, wearing a faded worn flannel shirt and a tied rope for a belt. His boots were newer and Sheila looked up from his feet to find him staring at her.

"I'm working on the shutters. Martin is in charge here," and she nodded toward the boy who stood frozen, staring.

"Yes, ma'am," the Marine said softly and then smiled at the boy. "Just need some water," he said and held up an old metal canteen.

"Yes, sir!" Martin almost shouted, and Sheila smiled as the boy ran to the first table with a pitcher of water and then waited for the man to follow.

Sheila watched for a minute longer and then moved to the kitchen to check on the vents and shutters there.

Jeff Wimmer was sitting on a stool, crying, while Tommy Cosery patted his shoulder. They both looked up as she entered and Jeff struggled to wipe his face as the tears continued to fall.

"It's ok to cry," Sheila said and walked past them.

173

Jeff was never very smart or focused, and his brother Pete looked out for him when they were in school. Sheila had always liked Jeff. He was a good artist and spent most of his time watching flutterbys in the sky. Pete kept him from getting bullied by being the biggest bully of their class, and Sheila pushed down a moment of pity for the man as he blew his nose on a kitchen towel behind her.

"Oil for the shutters," the Marine said, and Sheila turned to see him now standing in the kitchen doorway.

She glanced around, spotted a pot of pan drippings and picked it up, moving toward the door and daring the man to block her way. He stepped back and through the doorway as she approached, leaving a hint of campfire and sweat in his trail. She walked past him and toward the first window.

"Don't," the man said as Sheila pushed a chair closer to the wall and climbed up. She paused and frowned at him.

"Turn the crank after I add the oil," she said. It was a reach to get to the hinge, but she dipped two fingers into the grease and stretched up carefully to slather the top, before hopping down. She pushed the chair with her knee, not being willing to put the grease pot down or use her dirty hand to move the chair. Climbing up, she greased the second hinge.

The Marine waited until she was back down from the chair before he turned the crank. The protesting metal slowly shifted until the shutter was closed tight, and Sheila wondered if the grease had helped or if brute strength had done the job. She moved to the second window and then thought to look for a nearby chair. The Marine brought her chair with him, carrying it one-handed as he scanned the room.

They were behind the cafeteria door and Sheila climbed up the chair as Ell Menedez and Tracy Waters walked in.

"Not skinwalker," Tracy said, and Sheila got the impression of an involved conversation.

"My dad said they were telepaths, read your mind, make you believe them," Ell Menedez answered as they stopped at a table.

Sheila reached up to grease the first hinge.

"I know!" Tracy exclaimed. "It can't be coincidence. They have a plan," the other woman said as Sheila climbed down from the chair and the Marine lifted it and put it under the second hinge silently.

"The elders don't speak outside of the cemetery," Ell said, and Sheila frowned as she climbed up to grease the second hinge.

"Patty said Waits killed Cosery," Tracy said.

175

Sheila climbed down from the chair and turned to see if either of the two boys was within hearing of the women. Tom was still in the kitchen with Jeff, and Martin was standing at a table, pouring syrup into bottles, listening to the women talk with an angry frown on his face.

"We don't know where they were," Tracy continued, and Sheila started to step toward the women when she saw Martin put down the syrup jar and move around the table toward them

"Let him fight his demon," the man beside her whispered.

"Why would the elders tell us to trust them? I think they are telepathing us to make us trust them," Ell said and it seemed like an agreement as Tracy nodded her head.

"I think gossiping is mean and rude," Martin said. "My teacher told me only stupid people gossip because they don't have anything to talk about," the boy finished saying as he walked past the two women to approach Sheila and the Marine. "Thank you for helping with the shutters."

The Marine nodded and turned to crank the second window shutter closed without comment.

Sheila turned away from the two women and smiled to Martin before moving to grease the third window's hinges.

The women were silent as they walked out of the cafeteria.

\#

The pile of wood and wet hay looked like enough to smoke several young pigs and Chief Jessup Tranger was certain it wouldn't last the hatching.

"Pull boards off of the inside barn walls. You need more wood," he said to Tammy Toms as the woman poured more water on the hay.

"I have six hours yet," was her response, and Jessup looked at the sky to confirm the time.

"Call me if you need anything," he said as he moved to leave.

"Answer your damn C&C occasionally," Tammy replied and then smiled.

They had dated, talked about marriage, years ago. Before he was asked to be assistant chief by acting Chief Cherry Pyle when the rot turned Chief JJ Toms into a sleeping statue and Tammy told him she saw no reason to remain involved with colony politics. Her brother's death had ended their relationship when Jessup stepped up.

"Hey, Chief," Toni called out as he jogged toward him and Tammy. The youth skirted the pile of wood that would be a smudge fire and stopped beside the hay bales.

"What's up?" Jessup asked the teen who looked years older than the day before. His smile was gone, his eyes were almost squinted shut, and he seemed to try to watch the tree line and the fields all at once.

"Alec said to find you; there's a problem," Toni said, and Jessup pulled his C&C out of his pocket as he gestured for the teen to walk with him away from the barns and onto the path toward the East, where he had sent Beth and Alec to clear out houses of grubs and the dead.

Jessup scrolled through dozens of messages from people who weren't actively working during the crisis until he found Alec's last message. The time stamp was twenty minutes past and Jessup glanced to see if Toni was sweating or winded. The teen was tired, licking his lips, and trying to watch everywhere in a paranoid way that wasn't productive. Jessup stopped, offered his water, and thumbed on the message to listen.

"Hey, Jess, I need you to see this, um. Peters' back field. It's pretty bad." Alec's voice was quiet and Toni winced at the message.

"We can cut across the orchard," Jessup said and gestured off the path.

Toni paled, shook his head no, and swallowed without saying a word.

"Let's go," Jessup said and started jogging slowly on the trail, taking the long way.

Two miles out and they were approaching the orchard on the rock path to the South side of the ridge when two of the Marines joined them. Any thought Jessup had entertained about slowing down to rest was pushed back as he struggled to maintain his slow pace without losing his breath.

The vineyard came into view through the trees and they made their way alongside it until the vines were replaced by wheat and Haily Peters' house on the left.

Jessup could see Alec and the twins standing on top of the two-story broken-rock ridge that the Peters family mined for gravel. The rock was in the afternoon shadow of the forest. The East Ridgeline was shorter than the West Ridgeline and he could hear the waterfalls on either side of the farm as a faint hiss that bounced off of the trees and seemed to have no source.

"Careful, Chief!" Alec called down as the runners slowed at the base of the rock and Toni scrambled up.

The Marines stood, silent, watching their surroundings, while Jessup struggled to not double-over and forced himself to climb the rock.

The sound of a Marine, climbing beside him made Jessup aware of a different noise. A wet sliding, slapping sound that was punctuated by a popping and a crack at regular intervals. It was coming from the other side of the rock. He reached for a new handhold as he moved up the rock.

Someone standing above shifted and gravel fell between his face and the rock wall as Jessup forced his tired legs to push him higher. A weather-worn hand appeared in front of him and he accepted the help as he climbed to stand on top of the rock.

Alec met his questioning gaze without comment and turned so he could step forward to see the other side of the rock. The hiss of the waterfalls was lost in the roar on the other side of the ridge.

From a few feet off the base of the rock until they were lost among the hunter trees, the ground writhed. Dusty blue-green and streaks of black and red. The ground was a solid mass of six-inch worms that moved from the forest's shadow to a freshly-tilled field on the North edge of the ridgeline where the sun touched the open ground. The worms moved into the sun, lay still for a moment, and then popped into a ball that hardened into a black shell. Thousands of black shells lay between the trees and the ridge, and Jessup realized that the shadow line was moving slowly into the field as the day went by, and then his brain processed the thousands more broken shells scattered in the field far past the current shadow line.

Watching, Jessup saw one black ball crack open and a small blue and green bug crawled free, sat for a moment in the sun, drying, and then burrowed into the ground and was gone.

He looked back over the thousands of worms making their way from the trees toward the sun line.

"Dynamite," a Marine said and then coughed against the hoarseness of his throat.

Alec reached into his pocket and lit a blast cap, throwing it toward the black balls in the field.

The percussion stopped a thirty-foot circle of worms and the men watched silently as more worms swarmed over their dead without notice.

"Three days are lost. The skinwalker needs fire when the red moon returns," a spirit said from in front of Jessup. The swirl of dust and wind was hanging in midair.

"Three days from now?" Alec asked.

"Why don't the trees get them?" Toni demanded.

"You do not eat fleas," the spirit said and started to fade away.

"How do we join you at the fire?" the Marine shouted, his voice hoarse and raw.

And the spirit swirled back into form.

"Five, maybe seven, but only two who can talk."

"Fuck."

"Behind your eyes."

"We need intel."

"Talk to yourself who is lost."

"How long before the swarm?"

"Listen to us. Join us."

"We want to save these people. Her."

"You want to save yourself."

"Please," the Marine whispered, and Jessup watched the man stare down the spirit.

"Three days are lost. They will dive into clean fire. Do not flood the fields. You will not win for your losses. Jacob RunsLightly is ours." And the spirit was gone, the dust falling away on the breeze.

"The red moon rises tomorrow night," Toni said, and Jessup turned to watch the worms move toward the sunlight.

"Get more blasting caps, kill as many as you can," Jessup said.

Chapter 13

Projected Earth date: 2132

Planet Date: 0105, Mid-Warm

Coyote's Winter House, Rex Tyrol, Designated
Choctaw Emigration planet, Kanto Corporation

"Chief, I got one can of imported powder left
and a bucket of Petey's crap," Alec said over the C&C.

Jessup had grabbed his old C&C from his
office; sent key people the number as a way to block
out the missing-dog-hysterical-mom calls after Shelly
Pyle wasted thirty minutes of everyone's time searching
for her youngest kid only to realize that it was the dog
she was missing and she lied to get priority. The dog
had been safe at the neighbors' the whole time.

"I'll send Wayne with more powder," he
replied. He was walking around the colony, unable to
just sit at his desk and wait for nightfall. He wanted to
see people more than he wanted to be seen.

"Dynamite," a Marine said, and Jessup didn't look over to see the man now walking beside him, again.

They came and left, moved between buildings and jumped down from roofs unannounced. Chief JJ Toms had championed the few remaining Marines right up until his death. He argued that they were a part of the colony as much as any immigrant. And that their eccentric behavior that often leaned toward drunken fights that broke jaws and bones and sometimes skulls was a result of the same programmed reflexes that had saved the colony before. Nine Marines had silently carried Chief JJ's rot-created statue out to the cemetery and placed him on a slight hill overlooking the river to the Northwest side of the colony. And the next morning only Westover remained in town, refusing to explain where they disappeared to, or why. Jessup had pushed for an answer and Westover only said, "They're still here, just don't see anyone worth talking to anymore," and walked away, moving his housing to a small abandoned cabin from the second colony.

Now they were back. Jessup didn't know how many Marines there were as they all wore similar faded clothes, though the one beside him had a pair of boots that he knew were stolen from a porch three years ago.

"Hasn't been high explosives in a supply ship in over a decade. I think Beth has a few loads in the Armory. Tammy might have some at the barns, but mostly we have powder from stripped ammo and a few guys make old-fashioned powder for fishing," Jessup said without addressing the man directly.

The Marine walked a few more steps and then turned around and jogged back toward the town center and the Armory.

"Marine coming your way; give him any explosives in the armory," Jessup said by way of hello when his cousin Wayne answered his C&C.

"Beth gave them full access to the safe. Two guys have been here all day, stripping rounds we don't got guns for and making pipe bombs," Wayne replied.

"Good," Jessup said with a near smile. "Make sure they eat," he added without thinking, and then paused, trying to remember when he himself ate last.

He thumbed off the call and dialed Tammy.

"Hey, give the Marines any high-explosives you have," he said when she answered.

"Fuck you," was her response and she cut the line before he could reply.

He redialed and walked as he waited for her to re-answer.

"Fuck you," she said again. "The explosives were the only thing that worked last time. My brother blew the fucking bugs to hell. I'm keeping my stash for the animals," she finished and cut the line again.

Jessup stopped, glanced down the path toward the Northwest tower and watched a spirit move on the wind in front of him.

He heard the echo of the dog spirit bark twice from the tower and decided to survey the area.

As he walked, he dialed Westover.

"Tell them to leave the explosives at the barn alone," he said when Westover answered.

"They don't have radios," Westover replied.

"Don't fuck with me, Doctor, just think it at them," Jessup snapped. "That's why I called you."

"I already did, and they're going to put back some of the barn's explosives. Trey is staying with the sheriff kid's sister. We owe him," Westover said in a distracted voice.

It took Jessup a minute to remember that JJ had been the sheriff when the last hatching devastated the colony and the landed Marine battalion.

"Thank you," Jessup said and put his hand on the railing to start climbing the observation tower.

"Chief!" Westover said loudly and Jessup paused two steps up the spiral.

"Yeah?" he asked, looking around to see a lone Marine on the path approaching him at a slow jog from the South, and Bill Barnes and his older daughter walking toward him across their wheat field from the East.

"I… I'll be at my office if you need me," and the line toned out.

Jessup waited for Bill and Nina to get to the tower. The Marine arrived first and stood silently, watching the wheat field with a frown.

"Stick to the paths from now on, Bill," Jessup said as the older man leaned on his daughter and struggled to catch his breath.

"Answer your damn phone," Bill replied, his voice angry and blunt.

"What can I do for you?" Jessup asked in a business voice.

"I have two cases of Winchester Smokeless your gestapo never got. Figure you can use it better than me," and he held up a hand covered in rot. Bill was nineteen years on the planet and Jessup understood the concession he was making. The flat line of his daughter's mouth suggested that either it was her idea or she didn't agree.

"Rifle?" the Marine asked.

"We're keeping the rifles and loaded ammo," Nina said, staring down the Marine who never looked away.

"We're asking people with weapons to move to either the school or the barns," Jessup said.

"Chief. The power station never survives these things and I ain't going near the barns. Everyone knows how many grubs got in the last time. My wife's father spent his life breaking rocks to make a castle. You tell people we got room," and he turned to leave.

"There's a gargoyle up there," Nina added as she moved away, back across the wheat field with her father.

Jessup looked up the tower stairs before turning to the Marine.

"Do you want me to send someone for his powder?" he asked when the man didn't follow the colonists.

"We're almost there," the Marine said, and Jessup squinted to see two forms jogging toward the house from the cemetery path.

Three more people were crossing the wheat field, aiming for the tower above him.

"Hey, Chief," Beth said as she, Bob, and Terry approached, and Jessup frowned that she had crossed an open field.

"Fields aren't safe," he said and looked back up the tower stairs, trying to decide if it was worth climbing up to see who died.

"Good to see you too," Terry quipped, and Jessup frowned at the teen.

"We were headed for Bill's. Records say Chief Toms let him keep some powder as a security blanket. Hoping he still has some left," Beth said with an equally stern frown at her companion.

"He offered it. Marines are fetching it now," Jessup said and felt a sudden ache deep in his chest. A heartsick grief and anger that left him nearly breathless and he glanced quickly at the Marine, thinking it might be a telepathic projection of some form.

"Shit!" Terry exclaimed and Jessup saw the Marine squint and watch the teen. Terry was third generation, nineteen, and healthy with a history of fights and disciplinary actions. "How the hell are we supposed to defend ourselves if they keep taking the guns and ammo?" Terry demanded, waiving his hand at the silent Marine and addressing Beth.

"They are going to defend us," Beth said. "It's their job."

Jessup continued to watch the Marine study the teen like a maggot on a biscuit.

"Fuck!" Terry said again and turned to leave.

"Stay on the trails," Jessup said louder than he had planned and the kid shot him a glaring look before walking South on the path.

Jessup turned to the Marine and asked bluntly, "Was that you?" without explaining.

The Marine stared off into space, his lips moving occasionally as he had a silent conversation, before blinking, refocusing on Jessup, and gave a single tight head-shake no.

"What?" Beth asked, staring from Jessup to the Marine and back.

"Kid's an active empath," the Marine finally said out loud. "Seems to be jacking the hot-link. Shouldn't be possible."

"The bugs?" Jessup asked, in shock at the admission.

"No," the man replied. "Maybe the trees."

"Or the spirits?" Jessup probed.

The Marine's eyes drifted to some spot a few feet behind Jessup and then snapped back to his face for a moment.

"The kid's an active empath. We've spotted several. Westover is checking the sperm bank and we're ignoring them until after the bugs are gone," the Marine said mechanically, and Jessup frowned and nodded to Beth, indicating that they should start walking on the East path toward the town center. The Marine continued to stare into space, lips moving without sound and not acknowledging them leaving.

\#

They're gone.

I can see them.

What was the kid's name?

After the bugs are gone.

You should have asked his name.

They're gone.

The farmer can see you.

Just get a visual, scout the area, and leave.

The drunk is a waste of time.

She said there was a statue.

The dead are a waste of time.

Get a fucking visual, and, for the first time in years, Westover felt his emotions push through the link.

Weistler climbed the tower two steps at a time and turned the corner on Patty, frozen in stone, most of her disarrayed bathrobe absorbed and now soft rock. One slipper missing, the toe box of the other as well. The woman sat on the bench, arms wrapped around herself, looking to be in the middle of rocking herself and eyes closed, tears and nose-snot gravel on her otherwise peaceful face.

Westover reached through the link and scraped at the tears and snot until her face was smoother.

Sandpaper, he thought as he looked down. *It shouldn't be possible. We're missing something,* he added, mostly to himself.

And a spirit coalesced on the bench beside her.

"We need to know how to join you at the fire," Weistler said out loud, and they waited.

The dog spirit barked, moved closer to Patty's form, and barked again.

Good dog, someone said and Westover was surprised that he didn't feel the comment coming. That it was a separate thought in Trey's mind.

The dog barked again and a new spirit formed.

It was Allans; still young. His hand freshly amputated, and not the rotten wound that had let the fungus into his body and ate him. Until he died and became a statue in the woods, standing next to Joab and Frenz as permanent sentinels.

Allans looking like the night the power station slid into the river.

The dog barked again and Allans met Weistlers' eye with confusion and not recognition.

We need better intel, go sit by the fire with the dog and then report, Phillips voice carried through the link, and Allans tried to salute with a bloody stump before turning to look at the spirit dog.

The dog barked and was gone and the dust that made Allans' form swirled once and fell apart.

"Something changed," Westover thought and Weistler said and everyone agreed.

After the bugs, was the consensus and Westover went back to studying his own records.

#

"Bug!" Loko shouted behind him, and Alec dropped into a crouch without thinking, lit fishing blast in his hand un-thrown.

The Marine beside him dropped to a knee, took the blast out of his hand, and threw it toward the mass of worms still leaving the forest. It detonated in the air a few feet above the worms and instead of killing a thirty-foot circle, the concussion killed almost a fifty-foot swath.

"Shit," Alec whispered as he realized that they could have been killing more worms for less powder. The sun was close to setting and the five hours he, the twins, Toni, and the lone Marine had spent priming and throwing blasting caps had not been wasted. The living worms were a solid carpet of blue gray from the forest into the destroyed wheat field, but thousands were also a dead and lifeless pastel gray that clogged the way to the sun and slowed the migration down, if only slightly.

"A bug just crawled out of the ground over there," Loko insisted, pointing toward where the field met the Peters' gravel yard.

Alec accepted a hand up from the Marine as they both turned to watch where Loko was pointing. Alec let his gaze slide over the burnt farmhouse and the slaughter he knew was inside. The Peters family spent years building out the gravel and rock yard as a buffer from the grubs. They had installed heavy metal shutters and replaced all of the wood doors with recycled aluminum. They'd traded rock for heavy glass, and seemed to have done everything right.

Except for the dogs' door at the back of the kitchen, there was no easy way into the house for the bugs. Old man Peters was an immigrant, five years on the planet when the bugs hatched last, and Alec could barely remember him telling stories of wood doors eaten and glass windows broken by the swarm. Like many others, he had devoted his life to making his home bug-proof, even though he knew the rot would take him long before their return.

And now his family was dead in their rooms. The house was a smoking shell; burned to kill the grubs that were unable to find a way back out of the all-you-can-eat buffet of trusting walls and thinking there was another year before they needed to worry.

Alec watched as a second beetle, round and shiny and nothing like what he had been warned about, crawled out of the ground and sat shaking its wings. He felt relief flood through him, almost laughed, as Moko reached over and slapped Toni's arm in irritation at the emotion.

The Marine squinted in the setting sun and looked from the bug to Alec and then to Toni as the younger teen blushed.

"That happen often?" the Marine asked, and Alec watch the bug fly away before turning to answer for his friend.

"Third generation," Alec said, thinking the man would understand that the kids either died young or had rock calluses and either way were halfway to telepaths and annoyed the shit out of their friends with the oversharing and honesty.

The Marine nodded and turned to watch two more beetles crawl out of the ground at the edge of the field. One flew toward them in a lazy buzz of oversized wings.

"They shed the outer shell," the Marine said and used his stickball club to knock the bug back into the field, dead. "Time to go."

"We've still got blasts to throw," Toni protested, and Alec could feel his disappointment.

"We take the ordinance and we move," the Marine insisted, and Alec looked back toward the Peters house to see a small swarm of bugs between the smoke and them, circling in the shadow of the trees, waiting for the sun to finish its slow setting.

"Let's go," Alec agreed, grabbing a half-full box and moving back along the rock ridge to climb down.

The worms had moved down the ridgeline until they found a gap and now the ground from the edge of the gravel pit to the main trail writhed as they climbed clear and stood looking out at their blocked path. More than twenty feet of solid worms moving on instinct toward the grapevines and the light of the setting sun.

"I don't see any mouths," Moko said in a near whisper.

The Marine moved to the edge of the gravel and reached his club slowly toward a mass of worms. One spun about and hit the side of the club, leaving a black smudge of goo on the wood. The Marine stood, and stepped back from the edge.

"Paralyzes on contact. Grubs spit it ten feet," he said, and Alec didn't ask for details, just reached into his box and pulled out a handful of fishing blasts.

The Marine accepted the blasts and lit one to throw at the edge of the gravel. The concussion killed a ten-foot arc of worms, but the mass traveling from the South Ridgeline quickly filled the dead zone. The Marine watched the worms for a minute longer, then lit five blasts in one handful, nodded to the guys, and threw the blasts to the South side of where they stood.

The blasts detonated a few feet off of the ground, killing a large swath and for a moment, slowing the worms behind them, opening up a brief gap as the worms clear of the blast continued on their way toward the sun and the worms behind the blast worked their way through and over the dead worms.

The Marine ran across the gap and Alec followed without thinking. Loko and Moko grabbed Toni and the three barely cleared the gap before the worms climbed over their dead and refilled the area between the gravel pit and the path.

#

"Joab," Westover said and focused on his memories of the short angry Marine who died of the rot three years after arriving on the planet.

He's dead.

Dipshit.

"Joab," Westover said, forcing his thoughts into the link against the others.

Doc, back off.

"Joab," Westover said, again and stared at a computer image of Joab and Michaels standing together, laughing.

They were lovers but the pressure of the telepathic hot-link had muted their feeling toward each other. While no one cared, and the occasional night of same-sex passion offered a relief from Trey and his nightly prowl for local women, the link removed any illusion of privacy and they drifted apart from not wanting to share their relationship with forty other surviving Marines in the mix. They lived together at the farthest edge of the hunter tree forest until Joab got the rot and everyone felt his pain. Michaels ate a bullet hours after Joab died, and Westover never let go of the guilt that he should have predicted the risk and drugged him.

Shut it down, Doc.

"Joab," Westover thought forcefully; he knew it was a matter of minutes before one of the five surviving Marines reached his office and interrupted him.

Can't a guy get some sleep? Joab asked.

It was the last thing the man had said before the rot bloomed on his chest and shoulder and covered his body in the wet black slime that turned people to stone.

Where's Michaels? Joab seemed to be in the link, Westover back-scanned for his body and found the statue where they had left it.

Well, fuck me. Damn, Joab looked around in the link. *Where'd everyone go? Colonel Phillips?*

Westover watched the Marine shift from confusion toward anger and fear as the link shifted from Trey's view of Sheila, on a ladder reaching for a vent string, to Metzger and Lonco carrying heavy boxes of gunpowder into the Sheriff's office, to Weistler jogging behind a group of local youth as they held to a path and aimed for the shuttle spire, to Phillips, smoking a long pipe with the assistant chief and two women.

"Doc?" Joab said and materialized in front of Westover. Confused and covered in rot.

The dust swirled and broke apart, reformed and fell. The spirit shifted from moments before death to younger, healthy, looking for a fight. And then he was gone, as a spirit and as a mind in the link that Westover could detect.

The others were silent as Westover changed the image on his screen.

"Frakes," Westover said and pushed into the link.

He broke his neck, someone said.

I need to know if it's the fungus, Westover explained.

After the bugs.

"Frakes," he repeated, and the others blocked him, not boosting the signal.

Westover sighed as he keyed in a different image to focus on.

"Frenz," he said, and the others pushed him out of the link, and then the dead Marine was in his mind and the link was back.

Report, Westover said in his best Phillips voice.

Fuck you, Frenz replied and materialized in front of Westover. The rot had swept through his body in days, after an abdominal knife wound that had become infected.

Now he stood in the room, pulling dust to him to form and using Westover as a mirror to change his appearance until he was clean and healthy, and possibly taller than he was in life.

Bet you made your dick bigger, too, Trey's voice said.

Report, Phillips' voice said before Frenz could reply to Trey, and Westover realized that none of his Marines had spoken.

I am no longer under your sorry-ass command, sir, Frenz said, and faded in the link while growing more solid in front of Westover.

The dust combined with ice crystals and his face was now solid-looking. He turned away from Westover to glide toward the door and the Doctor noticed that the image he projected was forward only and he hadn't thought to add legs.

I have more important things to do than pretend to be your bitch, Frenz added with an image of Kim in the control room of the power station leaking into the link through his words.

Subdue him, Phillips voice ordered, and Westover remembered that it was Phillips who used the man's own knife to slice through Frentz's stomach when the man was caught raping a young woman's dead body.

Should have thought of that before you summoned Jack the Ripper back among us, Metzger's voice said, but Westover could feel his Marines, separate from Frenz in the link, and silently watched the spirit.

Fuck off, Frenz replied and reached a skeletal hand out to open the office door.

The dust and ice wasn't strong enough to move the door and Westover felt the other man's frustration as he tried to dissolve and reform in the control room but couldn't. The link seemed to give him form and Westover's focus on him gave him a window to become solid.

The spirit turned from the door and moved silently toward Westover, broadcasting the image of shoving his hand down into the Doc's lungs and giving him the rot.

"I could use some help here," Westover said and thought about Patty's father in the tower.

"Here, boy!" Trey called loudly.

Westover scrambled to put a chair in front of himself. He was cut off from the door and on the wrong side of his desk, and he doubted his rusty fighting skills would work against a telepathically linked ghost made of dust and frozen air.

And for one moment the ancient tree mind overpowered the hot-link. Alien and bored and momentarily amused; it reached out, and then the dog spirit growled from beside Westover and an old native man stood in front of Frenz. The Marine spirit broadcast a thought of fear and irritation and then was gone from the link.

Westover swallowed, took a breath, and then felt the link solidify around his men.

The dog barked and he felt it brush past him. The old man's spirit fell apart.

"Wait!" Westover shouted.

The dog sat as the man's spirit faded.

"We need the light from the shuttle," Westover said to the dog and thought to the tree mind.

"You need to live," a voice said, though only the dog spirit could be seen.

"If you blow up the shuttle, half of the colony will be killed by the explosion," Westover insisted and visualized the two craters from orbit.

"If," and the tree mind stood just outside the link, staring at the orbital image Westover pictured.

Westover moved slowly around his desk and brought up his image archive, putting the orbital images on projection, using his far wall. Ten minutes of pictures and then tree mind left the link. Simply quit being detectable.

Westover scanned the men to see if anyone had moved. Phillips now stood directly outside his office, the others were safe, and Westover had a migraine.

Good work, Doc.

Phillips walked into his office.

"I shouldn't have called him," Westover replied, unwilling to say Frenz's name.

Dying of the rot lets you come back as a spirit.

"I'm not sure," Westover said bluntly.

\#

"Did you eat?" Beth asked as Jessup paused to drink a glass of diluted cherry juice.

"Tomorrow," he replied, mostly as a joke, but the truth was, he couldn't remember.

"Tommy, please get the chief two sandwiches," Beth said, and Jessup smiled and nodded at the boy.

The cafeteria was full of people, standing-room only where the tables were pushed together on the South side. It was also the school's gymnasium and someone had stacked the bench seats against the far wall, under the basketball hoop. Jessup scanned the room, looking to see who had come in, and trying not to think about the families who decided to trust their houses against the bugs.

The sun had disappeared behind the tree wall and the bugs had risen from the fields. Thousands of bugs moving through the colony in a swarm as the red moon rose in the sky and stained the valley with blood. There were crude jokes about the red moon rising every thirty-seven days and lighting the night for five days. There were reasons for the jokes as the second generation of women found their menstrual cycles synchronized with the red moon. Jessup glanced at Beth to see if she looked like she needed to rest. She would be angry with him if he asked, defensive, so he just tried to sneak a glance and then smiled at her when she caught him.

"I'm fine. Eat," she insisted when Jeff Wimmer brought them a plate, piled high with cold biscuits, cheese slices, and cherry tomatoes.

"I'm sorry it's cold, Chief, Miss Sheila says we can't run the ovens," Jeff said quietly, and Jessup barely heard him over the murmur of the crowd.

"Thank you for helping out, Jeff," Jessup replied as he took the plate. "Please tell Miss Sheila it's fine," he added when the other man didn't leave.

"I will," Jeff blurted and spun to move through the crowd at a near run.

"I thought he was smarter," Beth said, and Jessup chewed a bite while he thought about her comment.

"He was. In school," he agreed. He shrugged, and took a second bite. "Maybe that concussion he got two years ago?"

"That brother of his hits him upside the head all the time, that can't help," Beth said and they both turned to watch two Marines enter the cafeteria.

A third, the youngest-looking one, was already in the kitchen area, following Sheila around wherever she went and ignoring the whispers his attention to the young widow was causing.

The two new Marines came in fast and slammed the door closed, scanning for bugs that might have followed them in, before turning to look across the cafeteria. Jessup didn't need to turn to see the younger Marine in the kitchen door staring back at them.

"Is that Colonel Phillips?" Beth asked of the white haired Marine who entered the cafeteria.

"No," Jessup answered. The Colonel, the Sergeant Major, a Gunnery Sergeant, and two Lance Corporals were all that had returned from their seven-year exile. Jessup was obsessed with the Marines when he was a boy and memorized their names and ranks and used to follow Colonel Phillips around the colony. "That's Sergeant Major Metzger and Lance Corporal Lonco. Metzger's darker, Lonco has the scar."

The two Marines stood in front of the closed door and made no attempt to enter the crowd for food or water.

Jessup started to stand, to take them his plate, when Beth put her hand on his arm, stopping him, and pointed across the cafeteria to Jeff Wimmer. He carried two plates and a pitcher of juice while Tommy Cosery followed behind him with glasses and a towel. Jeff approached the Marines and pointed to the wall of benches where there was a nook between the end of the benches and the corner. Jessup watched the two men follow Jeff to the corner and place their war clubs on the top bench before accepting the food and drink.

They ate as if they were starving in half-sandwich bites and drinking a glass of juice at a swallow. Beth kicked him under the table and then gave him a look that told him to quit staring.

"Six more hours," Jessup said.

A muffled explosion sounded outside, and everyone turned to see how the Marines reacted. If it was something they weren't concerned about, it wasn't a problem. Only the Marines dropped their plates, grabbed their clubs, and were halfway across the cafeteria when a second explosion hit, large enough to rattle the window behind the shutters.

Jessup's C&C chimed as he moved to follow the Marines.

"Somebody's trying to blow the fucking airlock open!" Ross Senhass shouted when Jessup opened the line.

Jessup scanned the crowd to see Kim Bailey listening with everyone else. Kim made her way to him at the front door and the third Marine arrived just as the door opened from the outside.

Phillips and Westover pushed in and slammed the door, Westover slapping at the front half of a bug tangled in his weapon's carry strap.

A third explosion rattled the windows and Jessup heard broken glass behind the shutters.

"Chief?" Ross shouted.

"I'm on it," Jessup replied.

"Waste of demolitions," Phillips said.

"There's nothing on this rock that can get into a shuttle," Metzger added.

"Fuck you," Kim Bailey barked out. "I can make a boom big enough to take out that airlock."

Phillips turned from staring into space and met Jessup's gaze.

"So can I," Jessup replied.

"Yeah," Beth agreed in a subdued voice, and Jessup turned to question her.

"Six sticks of old man Peters' best lake-clearers are missing," Beth admitted.

"Pete stole those," Jeff Wimmer said and then hunched his shoulders to stare at the ground.

"You fucking goddamn lying-ass piece of shit!" Pete Wimmer shouted as he shoved through the silent crowd.

"He did. He used them all trying to clear some forest past the South river bend," Jeff added, and Jessup tensed, ready for a confrontation.

Pete cleared the crowd and charged toward his brother.

A spirit coalesced in front of Jeff and said, "A man turned to hate is a rabid dog to be shot."

Jessup watched Jeff nod once and then pull a small handgun from his pocket and aim at his brother, through the spirit.

"You fucking coward. Who the hell do you think you are?" Pete demanded, but stopped in his tracks as the spirit turned to dust, revealing the weapon pointed at him.

"Jeff," Jessup said, moving toward the man, but Beth put her hand on his arm and he saw her shake her head from his peripheral vision while Phillips stepped forward and partially blocked his path.

"I am going to beat your goddamn ass," Pete said and took a long step forward.

Jeff pulled the trigger, and his brother hit the floor before Jessup's ears quit ringing.

Westover knelt and placed a hand on the man's throat as the blood pooled on his chest.

"Let him die," Phillips said and turned toward the door as a fourth explosion rocked the building and the lights flickered.

"Oh Jesus, Joseph, and Mary," Ross whispered over the still-open line.

"Do you know who it is?" Jessup asked as Phillips opened the door and the Marine moved out of the cafeteria. Jessup and Beth followed before the door slammed shut.

The shuttle spire strobed in the sky to the North and Jessup took off, running to catch up as the Marines rounded the corner and disappeared. The red moon cast dark shadows and Jessup forced himself to ignore the small movements he glimpsed as he ran.

The door to the shuttle airlock was blown open and smoke billowed out. The strobe light from the spire clearly showed Jacob Waits being restrained by two Marines as a third stepped into the airlock.

"I am the acting chief of this colony! I order you to help me destroy this threat," Waits screamed before he saw Jessup. The look of shock on his face told everyone that he had believed Jessup dead.

"I saw you?" Waits said, blinking. "I saw you dead. Beth?" and he turned to Beth for confirmation.

Beth shook her head, confused, and looked at Jessup.

"The bugs got into your office. I saw you dead. Tell him, Beth." Waits continued to stare from Jessup to Beth, completely oblivious to the Marines holding his arms.

"No, Jacob," Beth answered. "Jessup's been with me since sundown," she added.

"But, you said blowing up the shuttle is our only chance," Waits insisted.

"We've seen a spirit take full form and then lie," Phillips said quietly, and the Marines released Waits.

"What?" Jessup demanded.

"Frenz is a spirit," Phillips commented, and Jessup felt stomach acid threaten to become vomit as he remembered the Marine who killed his cousin.

The hum of the shuttle engine shifted to a deeper throb and the strobe light flashed and then went completely dark.

"Ross," Kim said and tried to push past the Marine in the airlock.

"Door's fubar," Phillips said from behind her.

"Fucking emergency bypass protocols, moron," Kim snapped and shoved the solid Marine in the chest. The man took a single deliberate step to her left and Jessup moved to follow the engineer into the airlock.

The last explosion was inside the airlock; the interior door was torqued in its frame but still solid, and Jessup watched as Kim dropped to her knees in the middle of the chamber and pried open a panel.

A piston-driven pump bar sat deep in the recessed panel and Kim worked to move the mechanism. Lonco knelt and grabbed the bar with both hands and it moved slowly. With every pull up there was a scream of tearing metal, and with every press down, the left side of the wall pulled away from the interior airlock hatch until it was a three-foot gap. Kim jumped up to get into the shuttle.

The engines were louder and the throbbing shook the airlock. Jessup let Phillips move past him and then waited as the other two Marines entered behind Beth.

The smell of heat and steel hit him as he ran from the airlock to the control room and waited for Kim and Lonco to work the by-pass on the doors.

The gap opened and Frenz was standing in the way, on their side of the door. Solid and real and just as crazy as he had been before he died.

"You are always too late, Colonel," Frenz said in a voice that echoed from behind them.

"Stand down, Marine!" Phillips barked.

"Ooh, and you brought me a snack," Frenz said and moved toward Kim, without acknowledging Phillips.

Beth fired two rounds into the spirit, the bullets going through and ricocheting off of a wall to thud somewhere in the dark. Frenz's form puffed dust and then he turned to look at her with a smile.

"Wait your turn," Frenz said softly and continued toward Kim. Jessup looked around for a weapon as one of the Marines swung his club through the spirit. Frenz reformed with a shake of his head and a deeper smile.

"Hey!" Jacob Waits shouted, and Jessup turned to see him point an industrial fire-suppressor at the spirit and pull the trigger.

Frenz froze with a look of annoyance and then was gone as the vacuum sucked the dust and ice away. Jessup's ears popped as the system stopped. Phillips was frozen, staring at a spot behind Jessup, and the other Marines were glassy-eyed as their lips moved together.

"Oh, fuck!' Kim whispered from the gap into the control room.

Jessup moved to stand beside her and looked inside to see what was left of Ross, frozen in a permanent scream, turned into a gargoyle half-imbedded in a console.

"Can you shut it down," Jessup asked, and Kim moved into the room, checking dials, avoiding the compromised console.

"Oh," Waits said from the door, and Jessup looked over to see the other man leaning on the torn metal without regard to his own safety. Waits had aged twenty years and there was now a quarter-sized patch of black rot on his cheek.

Lonco pushed his way into the control room and moved to follow Kim.

"It's a bit tight in here, Chief," Kim said as she pushed past him to a different control panel and started flipping switches.

"Not yet," Lonco said and put his hand on her wrist.

"Chief?" Kim said, but didn't force herself free of the Marine.

"Explain," Jessup said, and the Marine moved his lips before blinking.

"The bugs are diving into the heat stacks. Couple thousand gone," the Marine replied and Kim lowered her hand.

"Five minutes," Kim said and moved about the crowded room, checking dials.

"Cut it as close as you can," Jessup said and pursed his lips toward the exit while making brief eye-contact with Waits and Beth.

"I won't blow us up," Kim said as Jessup stepped out into the dark toward the airlock.

Chapter 14

Projected Earth date: 2132

Planet Date: 0105, Mid-Warm

Coyote's Winter House, Rex Tyrol, Designated
Choctaw Emigration planet, Kanto Corporation

"Kids want to talk to you," the Marine said.
Sheila looked up from the fire to see him standing in
the kitchen doorway.

She had slept for a few hours after first dawn,
but nausea and people talking woke her just after the
sun rose above the tree line.

The shuttle was offline and people were waiting
for power to come back on as they sat around the
cafeteria and the school. Sheila had gone into the
kitchen, realized that the electric cook stove was
worthless, and set up a field kitchen in the teachers'

courtyard behind the cafeteria. It was a small, quiet garden with one table and a protected rose bush that was blooming in a wall of small flowers that scented the still air.

She fed bits of scavenged wood into the small rocket stove and waited for the water to boil for coffee.

"Please send them out," Sheila said and tried to make eye-contact with the man. He was the youngest-looking of the Marines, with streaks of gray in his brown hair and sun-darkened skin just starting to wrinkle.

He nodded without looking directly at her and then moved clear of the doorway to let Martin and Tommy Cosery out of the kitchen.

The boys held hands. Sheila smiled at them and waited as they stepped into the courtyard and then froze.

She sighed, took her water off of the fire, and stood to move toward the orphans. The nausea returned, and she paused, waiting for it to pass, before she smiled to the boys once more and then glanced quickly at the Marine to see him staring blankly at a spot to the left of her face.

"What's wrong?" she asked Martin when she reached him and knelt down to be at his eye level.

"Mister," and the boy took a deep breath, his brothers face was stained with tears. "Mister Waits never came to the cafeteria," he said in a whisper.

"He had a long night," the Marine said from above them, and Sheila looked up, before focusing back on the boys.

"I'll call him," she offered and reached for her C&C.

"He doesn't answer," Martin said.

"We called," Jeff Wimmer added from the doorway beside the Marine.

"Well, then," Sheila said and stood slowly, the nausea blooming into dizziness that passed before the Marine could take the three steps to be by her side. She accepted his offered hand anyway. It was a warm anchor while she struggled to focus.

"You three keep working in the cafeteria. People need to eat, and I'll go check on him with Mister...?" and she waited for the Marine to give his name.

The man blinked several times and then held up his unclaimed hand and looked at a scar that ran across the back from his thumb to his wrist.

"Lance Corporal Andrew Trey, Ma'am," he said and almost smiled, his eyes moving from the empty place and met hers for a moment before drifting back out of focus. "You can call me Trey," he added as an afterthought.

"Trey and I will go find Mister Waits and remind him to come in and eat," Sheila said and then she moved toward the kitchen door. "Oh, Jeff, please make sure my fire is safe," she added as she pulled her hand clear of Trey's and straightened her sweater.

"Yes, Ma'am," Jeff said behind her and Sheila walked through the cold, dark kitchen and into the cafeteria.

People turned to stare as she and the Marine made their way to the front entrance. The whispers started even before the door closed behind them, and Sheila ignored Ell Menedez's questioning look as she moved away from the cafeteria entrance and toward the school doors.

"We'll check his office room, then the main administration office, before walking to his house," Sheila said.

"He's not in administration and he wasn't at the school at dawn," the Marine said as he walked a half a step behind her and his eyes scanned rooflines and bushes. "We left him at his house just after first dawn," he added.

Sheila stopped in her tracks and turned toward the Marine.

"We left him?" she asked.

"Yes, Lonco and Weistler took him home after first dawn, when the bugs eased up. He looked sick with the rot," Trey said, and Sheila thought it sounded like he just processed the information.

"He's only three years on the ground." Sheila moved to walk back along the path, beside the stickball field and then toward Waits' house.

"Doc is joining us," the Marine said and they continued walking the half mile in silence.

Westover was at the front of Waits' house, looking like he had run too far, and Sheila realized that the man must be ten years older than any second generation man on the planet. The immigrants, like Waits, came in all ages; a third died within five years of landing, others lasted ten but they were hard years, full of pain from the rot. Those that died early seemed to get all of the pain of a decade of infection in a few short days, and Sheila was fearful more for the two orphan boys about to lose their surrogate parent than for the man she suspected was dying.

Sheila watched Trey reach into a pot beside the door and remove a hidden key without searching. Each new batch of immigrants included a thief or two and locking doors in the small colony was common. The fact that the Marine knew where the key was didn't give Sheila pause as she thought about the men moving through the colony with twenty-six years of disassociated boredom. She smiled as she thought of the plate of cookies she had once been accused of eating when she knew she was reading in her room.

The air in the bug-proofed house was thick and wet, and Sheila sighed as she thumbed on her C&C and called Chief Jessup Tranger.

"Waits has the rot," Sheila said when the line opened.

Trey came from the back of the house and shook his head as Westover started up the stairs. She felt Trey behind her as she climbed the staircase.

"I saw it last night, thank you," Tranger said in a professional voice, and Sheila thought he had decided she was gossiping.

She reached the top of the stairs and looked into the bedroom that Westover had entered and saw him standing just inside the room as Waits lay, struggling to breathe. The right side of his face was completely covered in black slime.

"Took you long enough," Waits rasped out as Westover moved a step farther into the room, but was unwilling to get closer to the active and aggressive fungal bloom that was spreading as Sheila watched.

"Chief," Sheila said in a soft, sad voice, not wanting to say that the man in front of her was dying or that he had minutes, not years. Not wanting to burden him as he struggled to sit up.

"I want to be standing," Waits said, coughing black spores into the air.

"Get her out of here," Westover nearly yelled as he moved backwards, away from the cloud of spores that rose with Waits' activity.

"I want to be standing," Waits said again, and Sheila recognized the singular focus of someone about to die from the rot. Her own mother insisted on a bikini top and kneeling. Her father had tried to sit in his chair until the pain overwhelmed him and he died in a ball on the floor.

"Come on," Trey said and put his hand on her elbow, but Sheila jerked away and moved quickly around Westover to give Waits support as he got his feet onto the ground and worked to stand.

"Shit!" Sheila heard behind her as she concentrated on helping Waits to stand. People died from inhaling the rot as it bloomed on the dying. Immigrants died quickly. Second generation not as quickly, but just as dead. Waits was the fourth person Sheila had been in close contact with. The fourth person she sat beside and watched die from the fungus. None had killed her, though each time her calluses got worse for a while and she wondered how her son would handle the exposure in her womb.

"I want to be standing," Waits said again.

"You are standing, facing East, in your home," Sheila said loudly and heard her C&C line tone out as Chief Tranger disconnected.

"I want to be standing with my hands on my hips," Waits whispered as he fell back slowly to sit on the edge of the bed. His left hand on Sheila's shoulder pulled her down toward him at an awkward angle, and she twisted to free herself from his grasp.

She could feel the rot against her skin where he had touched her and she resisted the urge to rub at the spot.

"You are standing up, let me put your hands on your hips," Sheila shouted as she watched Waits flail his hands around. She caught his left hand and lowered it to his lap, his right hand followed and the man sat, hands in his lap, unaware and waiting for death.

"I am an elder," Waits said after several minutes passed.

"You are a good elder," Sheila said in reassurance.

"Worth more than a bucket of spit," Waits said.

"A bucket of warm spit," Sheila agreed and saw Waits smile as the rot flashed over and his entire body glistened in wet fungus.

"Can you hear them," Waits voice asked, and Sheila frowned to realize that it didn't come from the dead man's body in front of her.

"Four minds in the night," Waits voice said and the spores in the air swirled about Sheila as she stood, frozen.

Westover and Trey were in the doorway, the doctor blocking the Marine from entering.

"There's a Marine among the wolves," and Waits' spirit was gone, the dust and spores falling quickly without wind to stir them.

Sheila heard the house door slam open and footsteps on the stairs.

"Waits!" Chief Tranger shouted from the hall.

"Too late," Westover said and pushed against Trey to exit the room. "It's not safe," he added before the chief could enter.

Sheila moved away from the black form sitting on the bed and paused three feet from the doorway.

"Please get me some water to clean up," she said, making eye contact with Trey. He nodded and stepped backwards into the hallway. "I'm covered in rot," Sheila said to Tranger and waved for him to go down the stairs ahead of her.

"Waits?" Tranger asked from the bottom of the stairs before moving away from her approach and letting her walk toward the bathing room behind the kitchen.

"He can wait until after the red moon sets," Sheila answered and saw a bucket of water waiting for her.

"I'll have hot water and clean clothes in ten minutes," Trey said from behind the chief, and Sheila pulled her shirt up and off without caring that the chief would see her breasts.

As Tranger fled the house; Trey froze for a moment and then left for the water.

Sheila used a cloth to wipe spores from her hair.

#

"Women talk," Sheila said an hour later as Trey dried her hair with the last clean towel. They were still in the bathing room, he was still clothed, and she was trying to pull clean pants over damp skin without breaking contact with him.

The Marine was silent, his fingers untangling her long hair.

"My mother told me Colonel Phillips got her pregnant when my father couldn't," she said as she reached up and started braiding her damp hair.

He stood behind her and lowered his face until his lips rested on the top of her head.

After several moments of listening to him breathe, Sheila turned around and reached up to catch his face with both hands before he could straighten and stare off into space.

She looked deep into his eyes, tried to see his feelings or thoughts, and saw a shifting of expression that made her feel like they weren't alone.

"He was my mother's secret," Sheila said. "She wanted to marry him when my dad died," she added and saw the flinch.

"Ell Menedez told me that the tall Marine used to visit her when her husband was hunting," she said and searched for a response.

"Lonco," Trey said in a near whisper, and Sheila watched his chapped lips move for a moment past the words. "Bad genetics," he finally added.

And Sheila thought about Ell's oldest girl and the wet cough that kept her in bed at nine years old.

"Women talk," she repeated and slid her hands from the side of his face down to the front of his chest and the buttons on the rough fabric. "And we fall in love, and if you're not going to stick around then you need to leave now because I'm tired and I don't want to be alone."

She didn't say there would be someone else if he left her. The immigrants came in batches of four hundred men to every one hundred women and even with the shorter lifespan, there was a glut of men.

He reached his hands slowly up her body from her hips to her shoulders, and then lifted her chin with one hand and looked into her eyes with the same blank stare.

"You will never be alone," he whispered before kissing her forehead, each eye, and then her lips.

#

"Did he say anything?" Jessup broke the silence and asked Westover as the two men approached the cafeteria.

"That he thought he was worth more than a bucket of spit," Westover offered with a tired smile.

"Yeah," Jessup said and regretted the hostilities of the last election that pitted immigrants against second generations in screaming matches about needing experience when the bugs returned.

"He was definitely worth more than I expected," Jessup said and paused a few feet short of the cafeteria entrance.

The sun was low on the horizon. Alec and his team had been blasting the few worms still coming from the forest all day, and Beth had sent runners to every occupied house with the good news being that they only lost two households the night before.

Thousands of bugs had swarmed the white-hot power station shuttle thrusters during the night to be fried up before they realized the threat, and at first dawn, the sky was clear.

Jessup glanced around at the stickball field and the people gathered outside of the cafeteria and realized that they had three nights remaining until the red moon set.

"Anything else," he asked Westover.

"Four minds and a Marine among the wolves," Westover answered.

"Ross said a tree, a flutterby, and an elder around a fire welcoming him, and then wolves hunting outside the firelight," Jessup said and looked back from the field to see that Phillips was now standing beside Westover.

"It's all the rot," Westover said and walked away, past the cafeteria toward his office between the school and the admin building.

"There'll be six feet of snow next month," Phillips said, and Jessup worked to switch gears.

"Yeah," he agreed.

"Shuttle engine's fubar," Phillips said. "People need to start chopping wood."

Jessup stared at the small wisp of smoke coming from behind the cafeteria and nodded.

"Three days, after the bugs," he agreed. "I need to go talk to Waits' family," he added as Tommy Cosery stepped out of the cafeteria carrying a pitcher of water and offered it to a group of men.

"We have the watch," Phillips answered.

"Thanks," Jessup replied. "Three more nights," he added and then moved to follow Tommy into the cafeteria.

Chapter 15

Projected Earth date: 2132

Planet Date: 0105, Fall

Coyote's Winter House, Rex Tyrol, Designated Choctaw Emigration planet, Kanto Corporation

Three weeks later

"How's that look?" Chief Jessup Tranger's voice asked as Sheriff Beth Pyle turned the corner. She was hunched forward, carrying a heavy, canvas-wrapped bag of blasting caps and trying to keep the wind from blowing her hat away.

"What?" she asked, not quite willing to look up to see if her fiancé was at the top of the ladder that blocked half of the walkway in front of the cafeteria door or if he belonged to the boots she could see standing beside the ladder.

The wind had ice in it and the smell of imminent snow burned her throat.

"The siren; how does the siren look?" Jessup said above her and she took her hat off to look.

The wind caught her hair and blew it in a brown tangle across her face before she slammed her hat back down one-handed and tried to adjust the awkward carry of the canvas bag.

"Here," a Marine said and stepped away from the ladder, then reached to take the bag.

Beth looked at the man's face and identified him as Lonco as she handed over the heavy bag.

"Thanks," she said. "I was taking those to the Armory," she added, and the man nodded once, without looking at her, and turned to walk toward her office.

"Siren?" Jessup teased as she watched the Marine walk away. He climbed down the ladder and knelt to adjust the wires attached to a rusty hand-crank generator from someone's irrigation gate.

"Jealous?" Beth teased back before looking up at the rusty metal speaker box that Jessup had nailed above the door. "What is it?"

"A siren," Jessup answered, opened the cafeteria door, and gestured for her to go in first.

About sixty people stood around in the cafeteria, and Beth recognized most of the community leaders for the colony. The Sheriff's office was appointed by the chief, and she made a point for her department to stay clear of politics. Her Assistant Sheriff, Wayne Tranger, was chatting with a man from the Second camp, and Beth frowned to see him at a town meeting.

Jessup stood beside her, and Beth watched from the edge of her vision as he pulled his C&C out and thumbed it on.

"This is Chief Jessup Tranger. The C&C's are running out of batteries and this is probably our winter storm starting up," he explained and his voice echoed through the room from each individual C&C. "We have cannibalized the primary alert siren from the shuttle and it is now installed above the cafeteria door with a dynamo crank on the ground below. I will be testing this siren at noon, exactly, and it will be sounded at noon every day moving forward. Should the siren sound at any other point, it is an emergency; get inside. And kids, you cry wolf and you will spend the winter chopping wood. Everyone, conserve your firewood as much as you can, work on your snowshoes, and I'll see everyone after the storm." Once he finished, he checked the time on his C&C and then turned to check the time on a large metal clock on a table beside the cafeteria door.

Beth looked at the clock; eleven fifty-seven and ticking toward fifty-eight.

"Hey, Tommy, want to ring the siren?" Jessup asked and the boy shook his head no, in a panic.

Beth tried to smile encouragingly, but Tommy ran from the main room toward the kitchen with everyone watching. Jeff Wimmer followed him, and Beth caught Martin's eye, to have the older boy shrug to suggest that he didn't know why his brother panicked.

"I will," Martin said and stepped to the door.

"Good, it will be a cafeteria job," Jessup said and opened the door for the boy to exit.

Beth watched the clock and as the sweep hand rose toward the top, called out, "Noon," through the open doorway.

People followed Jessup and the boy outside and Beth joined the end of the crowd just as the siren started to sound.

Martin was bracing both hands on one side of the wheel and almost pulling himself off of the ground with each quarter turn, Tommy would have been unable to turn the wheel alone.

The siren sounded a bit like a bug swarm as it started to hum, and people glanced around uncomfortably before the sound increased and became a distinct metallic wail, growing in volume until Beth reached up to plug her ears.

She watched as Jessup gave the wheel two fast spins to see if it would get any louder, and then smiled down at Martin as the noise eased.

When the noise faded, people quickly moved back into the cafeteria and Jessup put his hand on her shoulder, trying to steer her inside when she would have continued to her office.

"I need you inside," he whispered and she frowned as she followed him.

"Can I have your attention," Jessup called out. "We need to know how far the sound reached, so if you could make a quick call home and see if it was heard, I would appreciate it."

Beth pulled out her almost dead C&C unit and called her brother Alec, only to see him in the crowd just as his phone went to message. She thumbed her unit off and waited for people to finish talking.

"If your house heard the call, please move to the left," Jessup said, and Beth watched as all but four people moved.

Only the man from the Second camp and two people from the river bend remained standing beside her, and Beth shrugged and pointed to Alec across the room.

"Okay," Jessup said as the people in the room finished shifting. "Any further business?" he asked.

"I nominate Beth Pyle to fill the position of assistant chief," a voice called out, and Beth froze.

"I second it!" another voice shouted, amid chuckles and some outright laughter.

Beth felt her heart pound and blinked rapidly as she fought to breathe normally. The idea terrified her.

"If there are no objections?" Jessup said and she felt her hand drop to her duty weapon.

"I fucking object!" Beth said and turned to glare at him. "I really fucking object and decline."

And the startled look on her fiancé's face eased her panic.

"Oh," Jessup said. "The record should note that Sheriff Pyle declined the position. Any other nominees?"

"Alec," Beth said, to herself, as her mind identified the voice that called out her nomination.

"Alec Pyle has been nominated," Jessup called out, and Beth looked over to see him grinning at her.

"I second that," the man from the Second camp said to Beth's surprise.

"If there are no objections?" Jessup said and Beth wanted to kick him for how pleased he looked.

"So, the chief and the deputy sheriff are family, and the sheriff and the sssistant chief would be family?" an old woman asked from the side of the room and Beth recognized her as a first generation who had campaigned for Waits.

"Yes ma'am," Jessup said, and Beth waited for the woman to protest.

"I'm good with that," the woman said and several people nodded.

"Be sure, we won't be able to have the election until after the melt in three or four months," Jessup said as people nodded to themselves.

Alec moved through the crowd with a frightened, puzzled expression and gave Beth a glare before turning to face the crowd.

A few people clapped and most smiled.

"Let it be recorded that Alec Pyle has accepted the position of Acting Assistant Chief until such time as the weather allows for a full colony election. If there is no further business?" Jessup asked, and Beth scanned the crowd again. "That calls the Colony council meeting; see you after the storm."

\#

Sheila watched Trey as he picked up pieces of the wood he had just spent the morning chopping and stacked it against her house's over-hanging eave. The storms fell young hunter trees at the edge of the forest. The trees were full of pitch and burned hot, even when wet, and Sheila was appreciative of the wood.

The planet was called Coyote's Winter House because it went from Fall to Winter in a week-long blizzard and then the cold lingered until Spring hit with a week of thunder and lightning and a warm rain that melted the snow. There was no Summer. Just three months of not raining and a bit above freezing at night with sweater-weather during the day to four months of too cold to snow day or night. The two seasonal storms brought the only clouds. The orbital year was seven-and-a-half Earth months, two hundred and twenty-two long days marked by thirty-seven day months. The sun always low on the horizon and the winter nights were twenty hours long.

Sheila tried to smile at the Marine stacking wood, but he never looked up to see her as he worked.

She heard a knocking from the front of her house and moved to answer her front door, leaving the back door open.

Phillips stood on her doorstep, a large box of jarred food held in front of him as he stared at a spot just behind her and to the left.

"Come in," Sheila said and stepped back to let him pass.

"Kitchen?" he asked and Sheila frowned.

"You know where it is," she said and followed him back. "Sorry, I don't have any cookies," she added as he set the box on her counter.

"Hammer?" he asked without looking toward her, just stood in front of the box and stared at the wall.

"Where my mother kept it," she replied and reached by him to lift a jar from the box, then moved to put it on a shelf.

He was still standing there when she turned back, but he had moved enough to face her.

"Your door needs fixed," he said.

"And my hammer and nails are exactly where you left them when you fixed my mother's rain gutter," Sheila said, staring straight at the man her mother had only told her about once.

Sheila watched Phillips blink twice and then move to the toolbox stashed underneath the small kitchen table. She could hear the ax outside as Trey chopped another round of wood.

Phillips worked in silence and Sheila moved to put away the rest of the jars of food. The Marines and a few colonists were working their way through the empty houses of the dead to box up and transport the food, blankets, firewood, fuel alcohol, and other necessities to those with less. Sheila was grateful for the supplies, as she had not gardened that year and her mother's cupboards were full of old food.

"I have extra blankets if anyone needs them," she offered into the silence as he set hammer to a second nail.

"We're Pro-gen," Phillips said and turned from the nailed-shut window to put the hammer away.

"Genetically modified to be telepathic," Sheila said to show that she understood.

"Genetically modified to give the colony a defense against the rot," he said and stood, staring at the wall again.

"Oh," Sheila whispered as the words lined up and her brain tried to process. "Oh."

"Westover set up the sperm bank," he added, and Sheila frowned.

"My mother didn't use the sperm bank," she stated as she watched his lips move while she talked. The sound of wood chopping stopped. "I didn't use the sperm bank."

He turned his head slowly until his face was aimed at her, and then Sheila watched as he blinked to focus and then met her eyes with a brief flash of concern.

"You're third generation," he said, and his eyes unfocused to stare behind her.

"So?" she demanded, wanting to reach out and force his eyes to meet hers.

"I knew your mother, but it was Weistler's sperm," he said in a soft voice.

"Your fucking doctor keeps good records," Sheila said and realized that her voice sounded more bitter than she felt.

"Genetics are tricky," Phillips said as if it was an answer.

"Tell me something," Sheila said and turned away from him to put a water kettle on to boil. "Do you guys have a score card?"

She heard him snort and glanced over to see a near smile on his face.

"We miss from time to time," he said and shifted to be directly behind her, his hands reaching up and massaging her tight shoulders.

"The sick kids," she said and set out two cups for coffee.

"That's Lonco, bad genetics," he said and, from behind her, for a moment, Sheila couldn't tell if it was Phillips or Trey talking.

"Oh," she said and stepped to the side and away from his contact, just to make sure of who was behind her. He dropped his head for a moment and leaned against the counter for a breath before straightening and staring, unfocused, again.

Sheila retrieved a small jar of cream from her icebox and set it on the counter next to the cups.

"Third generation are empaths," he said and walked out of the kitchen to her front door and left before she could think to call him back.

Her hand shook as she poured the coffee and added sweet lime and cream to each cup.

Trey opened the kitchen door and walked over to accept the second cup as she finished stirring in the cream.

Chapter 16

Projected Earth date: 2132

Planet Date: 0105, Fall

Coyote's Winter House, Rex Tyrol, Designated
Choctaw Emigration planet, Kanto Corporation

"Wait for my signal!" Kim shouted.

"I'll wait for you to be clear and standing," Alec
replied and watched the feet of the engineer shift to get
traction and push her farther under the old by-pass
generator engine.

"Right," she called back. "Try it now."

Alec stood, hand beside the ignition switch, and
waited until Kim crawled out from under the machine
and stood up.

"It didn't work?" she asked.

"Didn't try it yet, thought you should have the honor," he said with a wave to the ignition switch.

She shot him an annoyed look, wiped her hands off on her pant legs, and moved to stand beside him. Alec smiled and tried not to glance at her chest as she reached for the switch to power on the diesel generator that had been found among the ruins of the second failed colony. She shot him a second annoyed look as she caught his gaze and then turned the switch.

The generator sputtered, growled, and then exploded in a ball of vaporized fuel that blew Kim into his arms and both of them to the ground.

Loko and Moko ran to help them, and Alec wished for the Marines' telepathy so he could tell them to back off. Kim was twenty-two to his eighteen and he was thinking he might have a chance without his friends' help.

Kim moved away from him, one hand at her ear, rubbing, and he watched her poke at the generator briefly before shaking her head.

"Toast?" he asked.

"Burnt toast," she replied. "I can't fix it."

"Beer?" he asked.

And she turned to stare at him for a moment. Alec forced himself to hold her eye contact as she looked from him to his friends and back again with a smile.

"My place for the snow, you bring the beer, and leave your pets at home," she finally said with a nod toward the twins, and winked before walking away.

Alec watched her walk and felt his heartbeat try to keep time with her steps.

"Dude," Loko finally whispered after she exited the barn.

"You're engaged," Moko added.

"Yeah," Alec said with a nod and realized that he was grinning.

#

Trey brought in an armload of wood, and Sheila closed the door against the storm. The wind was dying down as the snow continued to fall. The only distinction between day and night was the red glow from the moon and the gold of the first dawn.

Eight times he heard the muffled sound of the siren at noon and Westover still had an antique wrist watch that kept Earth time. He used it to track planet time on a smudged, old wall chart.

Westover and the other Marines had taken over an empty schoolroom, and Trey stacked the wood they needed into Sheila's box. The smell of burning furniture made him scan the fire, only to see the fireplace in front of Weistler as his hand added a chair leg.

Eight days.

Should be over.

Tomorrow.

Doesn't look like it's letting up, Westover said about what they had seen from Trey.

Tomorrow.

"Do you want more coffee?" Sheila's voice echoed from the edge of his senses.

Yes!

"Yes, ma'am," he replied and watched another piece of a broken chair being fed to the small fire. He could feel the others huddled in a ball under six blankets, trying to share warmth, while Weistler had watch of the fire and he reached out with Weistler's hand to test the temperature.

Other colonists had moved into the school as well, and the Marines shared their wood supply until they didn't have any left and now burned the classroom chairs.

"I'm out of cream," Sheila said and he shifted back into the room to glance at her before looking down at the coffee beside his outstretched hand.

"Thank you," he said.

Just fuck her, Westover said impatiently and he felt Phillips frown.

"I made soup," she added.

The sound of splintering wood startled him and he closed his eyes to hear it better.

"…and biscuits," she said in a faint voice as he slid into Phillips body and watched Westover and Weistler run in front of him, down the school hallway toward another classroom.

Westover opened the door and snow fell into the hallway about their feet and he felt the Doc focus his mind, searching for people under the collapsed roof.

Lonco's mind focused as well and found nothing where eight people had been.

"…will say we're engaged," Sheila said as the sound of breaking rafters pushed him away from the collapsed room and he opened the next door.

"Colonel Phillips!" someone shouted from down the hall, and he shifted into Weistler to watch Phillips run faster to the school's main exit doors. And for a moment, everything went dark as the roof broke open and an avalanche of snow fell onto Westover and Weistler.

"...or I can," her voice echoed to the shouts of others as snow was moved and he lifted a child to her mother.

Sheila's touch was a shock as the urgency of the others faded and he blinked to find himself in her kitchen looking at tears on her face.

"The school roof is collapsing, I have to concentrate," he said and looked from her eyes to her lips, before deliberately closing his own eyes and stepping away from her touch.

Westover had a nasty gash above his left eye and Weistler was free of the snow and moving to pull a colonist clear as Phillips and Metzger guided people with a rope through the blizzard to the sheriff's small office. Lonco's mind gave the school one last scan for life before he shook his head to the deputy sheriff and moved out of the building.

Now fuck her, echoed through the link and he felt Westover use his hand to reach out and touch her shoulder.

The link faded back and he saw her turn to him and then step into his embrace.

The smell of burning soup caught his attention several minutes later and she pulled away from him slowly.

"You have the rot," she said quietly as he sensed Westover on watch and the others asleep in a warm jail cell.

"We all do," he replied and looked down at the small, wet mole on his left forearm.

"I thought you were genetically immune."

"Resistant," he said and accepted a bowl of white beans and potatoes from her. The smell almost woke the others and he heard his own stomach growl.

"Oh," she replied without eating her own soup.

"Are we married?" Westover asked with Trey's voice, and he forced his expression neutral to fight the frown he wanted to direct at the Doc.

Sheila turned slowly to meet his eyes and Westover moved Trey's face into a soft smile.

"Engaged," she said and moved back into his arms.

Chapter 17

Projected Earth date: 2132

Planet Date: 0105, Winter

Coyote's Winter House, Rex Tyrol, Designated Choctaw Emigration planet, Kanto Corporation

"Do you think there's a link between the bugs hatching early and the severity of the storm?" Alec asked.

Jessup looked up from the pile of papers he was working on and thought about the question.

"Yes," Westover answered.

"Maybe," Jessup offered.

"I read through the record almanacs and it never snowed for eleven days before," Alec said. "Not even during the first or second colony times," he added.

"One hundred and five years since the first survey," Westover said and handed Jessup two new pieces of paper to sign.

They were working on updating the colony roster, finding the voter records and medical files of the dead and preparing them for archiving. Filling out a single-page death record for each person lost. Four hundred and seventy-three lost to the bugs and the storm. Another eighty-nine unaccounted for and presumed dead. Jessup was also working on a guide for future hiefs that included assuming every fall was a hatching year and what to look for as warning signs.

"Bugs came out of the forest and we are dying." It was a quote everyone knew and no one had understood.

"The survey team projected the planetary orbit and tilt and listed the temperature fluctuation as within human tolerances, if on the cold side," Jessup said and put his pen down to look at the doctor.

"Humans tolerate the Arctic on Earth," Westover said and handed another paper to Jessup.

"They would have sent us more greenhouses," Alec said, and both men nodded and went back to their paperwork.

"Emigrant colonies are just a tax write-off for the Corporations. They just keep sending bodies down until you find all the dangers. Fucking cannon fodder,"

Westover said in a distracted voice as he filled out a new death certificate.

"How far does telepathy work? I mean, could you talk to someone on the other side of the planet? Or set up a relay to go around the planet?" Alec asked, and Westover's pen stopped moving as his lips started.

"Can't reach the Southern Ridge camp from here," Westover finally said. "Five miles, tops. Hot-link is short-band radio and just better than line of sight."

"Hot-link is telepathy?" Alec asked.

"No," Westover answered and handed a new death certificate to Jessup to sign.

"Hot-link telepathy?" Alec said again and looked from the oblivious doctor to an equally confused Jessup.

"Explanation, Doctor?" Jessup said.

"None of your fucking business," Westover said blandly as he shifted his pile of papers and started a new death certificate.

"The telepathy is developed through progressive genetic therapy," Metzger said from the doorway as he stepped inside and out of the freezing wind.

"You sign away your life and a bunch of government scientists get to play God with your DNA until they get a pattern that works. Could be they turn you into a frog, could be you grow horns and get stronger, and if you're really lucky they find your master code and you get to be genetically perfect. Stronger, faster, healthier, and telepathic," Westover said and Jessup frowned at the anger in his voice. "Mostly they turn people into bags of human soup and learn from the ways they die."

"Why'd you sign up?" Alec asked.

"I didn't want to die," Westover said and pushed the papers away from him.

"Death row," Metzger said and Jessup saw him nod.

"Fuck you," Westover said. "I was exposed to Moler-gen. Had about two hours to choose between Pro-gen and risking some civilian genetic surgeon fucking things up."

"I was on death row," Metzger said. "Took a mind-wipe and Pro-gen. Joined the Corps."

"The Colonel was exposed to Moler-gen during the Swedish uprising," Westover said.

"So was Lonco, before the Marines," Metzger said.

"Trey was stupid."

"Cocky."

"Stupid enough to believe the recruiter," Westover said.

"Weistler was desperate," Metzger said.

"We were all desperate," Westover corrected. "That's why you risk Pro-gen, you're out of options and trying for a Hail Mary."

Metzger nodded and the room went quiet as Jessup scanned the death certificate before adding his signature beside the doctor's.

"The hot-link?" Alec asked several minutes later.

"A physical implant in the brain that can be turned on for short missions to allow for full sensory communication," Metzger said.

"Why do the spirits call you a skinwalker?" Alec continued.

"The hot-link's primary purpose is to allow two people to body swap in a crisis. The Doc can slip into my body and render medical aid at my location even though he's a mile away and running to help," Metzger explained and Jessup watched Westover clench his pen and stare at a spot on the desk without commenting.

"Um, short missions?" Alec pushed, and Jessup tried to catch his eye to let him know to back off.

"Seventy-two hours. Maximum functional window is five days," Metzger said in his flat voice.

"What happens after five days?" Alec asked and Westover slammed his hand down flat on the table.

"Suicides, insanity, death," Westover said in a tight voice and stood, walking to the door.

"But, they left it turned on. How did you survive?" Alec asked.

Metzger opened the door and Westover stepped out into the cold as the other man turned back to the room, said "We didn't," and closed the door behind him.

"You need to learn tact," Jessup said.

"That was more information than they have ever shared with us," Alec said, and Jessup realized that the kid had been pushing deliberately.

"Yeah, it was."

"I think the bugs knew the storm was coming and hatched early," Alec said.

"Maybe," Jessup replied.

\#

"Higher," Beth said as Kim steadied the ladder for Jessup.

The cafeteria roof had collapsed with the rest of the school and they were moving the siren to the front of the Admin building.

"The sound has to clear the hospital roof to bounce off the tree wall," Kim shouted up, and Jessup tightened his lips into what he hoped was a smile.

"It clears Westover's office roof," he said of the two-room clinic the doctor set up between the school and the admin building.

The other side of the school was the Sheriff's office and then the bulk of the shuttle. In the two weeks since the snow stopped, the walks were shoveled, cut, or melted in the arc of the town square and the main walks were cleared a mile out. Cutting was the preferred method. The snow was dense and easy to cut into blocks that were stacked to line the sides of the path and used by kids to build forts on top of the buried fields. They knew the snow would last four months solid and it was now tradition to build elaborate mazes and stairways to snow slides, and giant snow bowls for sledding.

The winter months were for playing and oiling leather while drinking beer around a fire pit with friends. The saw grass was safely blanketed, the hunter trees were sleeping, and the river surfaces were frozen solid. The days were six hours of sun with an hour of dusk on either side of the twenty-hour night. The planet was safe enough to almost be paradise in the winter; a frozen, dark paradise.

Jessup shifted on the ladder and leaned over to push the siren higher, its cord dangling down to the manual crank below, as Alec hung over the edge of the roof and pulled up slightly on the rope they were using to stabilize the heavy speaker.

"Looks good," Beth called, and Jessup tested Alec's hold on the rope sling before letting go completely to pull his hammer from his back pocket and accept one of the pre-nailed boards that Kim was straining to hold up to him.

The sound of bugs surprised him and he straighten up to check the skyline, meeting Alec's wide eyed-gaze just as the siren moved into a wail and ran up in volume eighteen inches from his face.

Jessup dropped the board to try to hold his ears against the pain and looked down to see Westover finish cranking, look at his antique wristwatch, and then turn to leave. Beth had a startled, and trying not to laugh, look on her face as she picked up the dropped board and handed it back up.

"Told you to be more tactful," Jessup muttered to Alec as he finished nailing the board into place and looked down to get another board from below.

"He's still pissed at me," Alec agreed. "As bad as the fucking trees holding a grudge."

"You talk to the trees?" Lonco said from beside him and Jessup glanced up to see the Marine holding the guide ropes while Alec flipped upside-down, head still over the edge and stared out over the rooftops and away from the town.

"Naw, they're pissed at me, but we have a truce," Alec said, and Jessup hammered the second board into place.

"Alec figured out how to break a tree grab; they don't like fishing blasts," Jessup said.

Beth handed him up the last board.

"You talk to the trees?" Lonco asked and stared down to make eye contact with Jessup.

"I wouldn't call it talking, just tell them I don't taste good when I walk by," Jessup said and reached up to tug lightly on the siren.

"Do the trees ever talk back?" Lonco asked and looked from Jessup to Alec and back down before leaning forward and putting his hand flat on the top of the siren and shoving down.

The siren was solid and Jessup spun his hammer before sticking it into his back pocket.

"No," Jessup said.

"Yeah, a few times," Alec said and rolled back to look down and meet Jessup's eye. "They don't really talk, just push at me with boredom and hunger, and they think we're funny," he tried to explain.

"They think we're a joke?" Jessup asked.

"Amusing," Lonco answered. "We amuse them. Like pets."

#

Jackass, someone thought as the siren spun down and Westover shrugged to himself.

Back in his office, he lit a fuel stove and set his timer for air quality. The clinic wasn't vented for a stove and trial and error had shown him that the alcohol stove would warm the room to tolerable before he was forced to open the door for fresh air. Three cycles of stove versus door and the front room of the office was warm enough to doze in. Previous years, he had wintered in the back office, using electric heat and the school's bathroom.

The kid hears the trees.

Third generation.

Second.

They talk to him.

The kid isn't Toms, Westover interjected. He resented Alec and while he couldn't put a finger on why, the memory of Sheriff JJ Toms becoming Acting Deputy Chief Toms during their first winter was enough of a parallel to blame.

Who's his father?

Not Lonco, Westover replied and there was a soft laugh in the link that wasn't familiar.

Where's the list of Lonco's brats? A voice asked and Westover felt his men tense and look around inside his head and their own.

I'm still working on it, Westover replied as Frenz took form in the heat exhaust of the fuel stove.

The dead Marine looked around, closed his eyes, and Westover felt his mind invaded by a buzz and a howl and the impression of screaming in the dark as his world became pain.

He regained consciousness as Phillips opened his door and threw a bucket of water on the hot stove, extinguishing the fire instantly but billowing out a cloud of steam, and Frenz laughed as he solidified before disappearing from the room.

You alive? Phillips voice slid into his mind and Westover throttled a scream from the rawness of his link and the nauseating migraine that made the room dark and cold and fading away from him.

Doc! You in there? Phillips called again, stepped into his body, forcing it to open his eyes and swallow against the pain, and Westover felt himself refocused and in Phillips' body.

The heart was a problem, the ache sharp and constant, the knee was damaged but functional, he needed shower and sleep and the amount of alcohol in the blood stream was distracting, and Westover blinked to see Phillips in front of him and to feel his own pain again.

He got thirty names, Westover said at the memory of the mental invasion.

Map them.

Menedez kid.

Roget boy.

Why? Westover said in defeat. *They're dying. All of the names he got are third generation and dying of the rot.*

Let me see the names.

And Westover picked up a piece of paper and turned it over, checking to see what it was, and wrote the names down. He felt his men throw up their locations and consider who they could reach.

You said thirty.

Westover looked to the names he had written down and counted twenty-eight. He closed his eyes and replayed the memory, saw Frenz pull up a memory of him writing down those children he expected to die of the rot soon and check them against Lonco's list of offspring. The memory played out and he saw himself circle Shirly Cosery's name and put a question mark next to Tommy and Martin Cosery.

Fuck.

Damn, Westover agreed as he felt the men moving.

#

"Thank you," Jeff Wimmer said to Sheila as she brought the blanket into the house and he shut the door against the cold.

Jeff, Martin, and Tommy had moved into the bottom half of Jacob Waits' house for the winter, and Sheila tried not to think about the statue still sitting upstairs, waiting for spring thaw to be carried to the graveyard.

"Do you have enough food?" Sheila asked as Jeff stood watching her move about the room.

"Yes, there was a bunch here," Jeff replied and Sheila turned to walk toward the kitchen.

"Do you mind if I see?" she didn't wait for his answer.

The kitchen was clean, and well organized with only three bowls and cups in the sink waiting to be washed while a large pot of soup simmered on the stove giving the room the comfortable smell of beans and cabbage. Two trays of brown cookies sat on the counter, cooling.

Sheila stirred the soup as she moved past and she was looking in the pantry when the kitchen's back door opened.

"Cookies!" Tommy shouted as he followed Martin into the room and then froze to see her standing in the pantry doorway.

The boys were wearing pants, mud boots, and jackets that she suspected weren't warm enough. Tommy had two gloves and a hat while Martin had one glove and a hat that was too big.

"Close the door," Jeff said and offered each boy a cookie.

Martin closed the door while Tommy continued to stare at her.

"I don't like trees," Tommy said as he accepted the cookie without looking away from her.

"They can be scary," Sheila agreed.

"You have a tree baby," Tommy announced. "I don't like trees," he repeated when his brother hit his arm.

"Can you see my baby?" Sheila asked and put her hand on her still-flat stomach.

"No," Tommy said around a mouth of cookie. "I see an angry man. He wants to yell and scream and hurt me."

"My baby wants to hurt you?" she questioned and for the first time since her mother's spirit had named the pregnancy, Sheila felt doubt creep into her.

"No. The angry man wants to hurt me," and Tommy pointed at the steam from the soup pot where a ghost of a face moved, silently watching the room.

"Oh," Sheila exclaimed as Jeff slammed a lid on the pot and moved it off the heat.

"Open the door," Jeff said and Sheila saw Martin move quickly to open the kitchen door as Jeff moved to take the pot outside.

"It's the steam," Sheila said and then froze when the door opened to reveal the Marine Metzger.

"Problem?" he asked, moving out of Jeff's way.

"There was a face in the steam," Sheila answered.

"He wants to hurt me," Tommy added.

"The spirits need dust or smoke and moisture to form," Metzger said and prowled the kitchen.

"Spirits can't hurt you," Jeff said as he returned and closed the door.

"Yes, they can," Metzger said.

"Gramma will protect us," Martin said and put a protective arm around his brother.

"Your gramma is a smart woman," Meztger agreed. "Call her," he added.

Martin looked from the Marine to Sheila and she smiled encouragingly when she felt his question.

"Gamma," Tommy whispered and Martin closed his eyes for a moment.

The new spirit swirled about the kitchen and Sheila watched as Metzger poured a small splash of tea or coffee onto the hot burner.

The small old woman floated through the steam and knelt to stand in front of the frightened boys.

"The angry man wants to hurt me," Tommy whispered and Sheila heard the man's laugh from the ceiling.

She looked up to see the rot bloom across a crossbeam.

"Everybody outside," she said as the spirit of the old woman stood and turned toward Metzger.

"Give him a rope," the spirit said, and Metzger poured more water onto the hot stove to billow up in a cloud.

The rot spread quickly, a black mass that Sheila had never heard of being on anything not living.

"Get them outside," Sheila hissed to Jeff as the man stared up in horror at the face that formed as the black mass dripped downward, reaching out for Tommy. He picked up Tommy and moved quickly to grab the door handle.

"The door's frozen!" Jeff shouted in a panic.

"Your body is empty. Just stone to crumble and die," the old woman said as Metzger watched her and poured a little more water onto the cooling burner.

"You're not immune," Sheila said to Metzger as she moved to tug him toward the exit for the kitchen.

"The boy is a genetic dead-end," the wet ceiling said in a voice that screamed and howled in a whisper.

"You are dead," the old woman said, and Sheila tried to move Metzger again.

Jeff and the boys were trapped, forgotten at the kitchen's back door and Metzger was standing too close to the dripping ceiling to survive a bloom as Sheila felt her skin crawl from the amount of fungus in the room.

"There aren't enough humans on this planet to survive a dead-end," it whispered, and Sheila felt more than heard a thousand voices dying in pain from the rot.

"Humans aren't from this planet," the old woman said, and then she gathered some of the dripping fungus into her to become a more solid form.

Sheila stared as she filled out and then moved to adjust her shawl about her shoulders and looked up at the ceiling in pity and annoyance.

"They sent us to change the DNA of the colony. The boy is a fluke and should be put down before it breeds. There are too few survivors. We have to survive and conquer this planet or coming here was a waste of good men and friends." The ceiling mass dropped down onto the kitchen counter in a solid ball and then slid to the edge and stood as a man.

Jeff and the boys were directly behind him and the old woman was between Sheila and Meztger and the angry spirit.

"There are fifty-five hundred colonists, Frenz," Meztger said, shrugging off Sheila's grasp and stepping forward.

"They quarantined the planet!" the spirit shouted, and Sheila watched the black glisten and shift.

"Your fear is as hollow as your threat," the old woman said, and Sheila realized that she was taunting the dead Marine.

"They send a new batch of immigrants every five years. Clockwork," Metzger said and stepped back to put his arm in front of Sheila and push her toward the open pantry door.

"They abandoned us to rot!" the spirit howled as the fungus swept across his form in full bloom.

The spirit of the old woman spread her arms like wings and stepped forward to engulf the black form as the bloom failed to find a body to transform and exploded with a scream.

Sheila watched the old woman shrink back and move slowly toward Martin and Tommy.

"You go outside until the rot fades again," she said in a soft voice, and Jeff opened the door easily.

"He left his body to crumble," she said, and Sheila felt like there had been a conversation that she missed as Metzger nodded.

"Auntie," Sheila said softly.

"The mother of Jacob RunsLightly," the spirit answered.

"Tommy said I have a tree baby. Why do you know his name?" she asked.

"Your son can see the fire; he will drive off the hunters." And the edges of the woman's form crumbled away.

"The trees?" Sheila asked.

"No child, the insane and empty. The hungry and the lost who cannot see the fire to join us. Your son will stoke the fire bright and drive back the night."

And the form of the old woman broke apart and fell in a cloud of fungus. Metzger grabbed her and pushed them both into the pantry, slamming the door as the cloud of rot bloomed outward.

The space in the pantry was not enough for two adults to be modest and Sheila relaxed into Metzger's arms as he held her in the dark.

Chapter 18

Projected Earth date: 2132

Planet Date: 0105, Winter

Coyote's Winter House, Rex Tyrol, Designated Choctaw Emigration planet, Kanto Corporation

"Jeff Wimmer has a big mouth," Beth said, and Alec nodded with a mouthful of oatmeal.

"Ell Menedez is blaming the Marines for her daughter's death. It's stupid. You ready?" Beth spoke while moving about the kitchen, moving things and wiping clean counters.

"Yeah," Alec replied and set his bowl on the floor for their small dog to finish. Jelly was a third generation terrier who came from solid Rez dog stock, and Alec missed her the weeks he spent at Kim's. Had been too distracted to notice that he missed her, but now that he was back in his own home, he realized and felt a pang as the dog leveraged herself up and limped

across the room to eat the food. Her back hips had the
rot and Alec took a moment and prayed that she would
last to see one more spring or go quickly.

Kim had a scrawny husky puppy she named
Berkers that loved the snow and argued with him about
the covers. Her dog was second generation and mostly
purebred. It was a planet designed for huskies and Alec
made a note to himself to include that observation when
the next immigrant ship came. To also note that the
planet should be shifted to emigration by Northern
Earth natives; Alaskan Natives, the Inuits, and not river
people like his own Mississippi Choctaw.

The main river to the North was more than a
mile wide at the narrowest, no one knew how deep, and
in the hundred years since landing there was no record
that anyone had tried to take a boat onto it. The
moogies kept them cautious on the banks and Alec tried
to think if he had ever heard of anything bigger in the
rivers. The Southern rivers were much smaller and
traveled in the opposite direction as the main, and had
semi-permanent portages established. He shook his
head, patted Jelly softly, and moved toward the kitchen
door.

"Your fan," Beth said and pursed her lips and
looked toward his ceremonial recreated eagle feather
fan that lay on the counter next to his folded sash of
office.

"Oh yeah," he said.

"You don't have to wear it," Beth said as he moved back to the door with the fan and sash she had made him during the storm.

"Seems pompous to wear a sash for four months," Alec said.

"Chief Toms was only sheriff for twenty-nine days before he became assistant chief, and he wore a sash for sheriff his whole life," Beth replied as they moved out of their yard and onto the path to the town center.

"Chief Toms stepped up in the middle of the hatch and saved the whole fucking colony," Alec snapped. His sister wasn't the first person to compare him to his childhood idol.

"You did pretty good, yourself," she replied. "Besides, you'll be assistant chief for a while. Jessup is healthy."

"There will be a new election in the spring," Alec reminded her.

"People will vote for you," Beth said.

\#

"We ought to have the election right now and boot the whole council!" someone shouted from the back of the room, and Alec glanced around looking for his sister.

During the winter months, a weekly town meeting took place after the Sunday prayer meeting and before the weekly social. The winter meeting tended to be about food and fuel supplies, accusations of stealing and paternity, and discussions of how to help those who had miscalculated their supplies to get through the cold. The winter meets were normally held in the school cafeteria and with that gone, today's meeting was inside the cargo bay of the dead shuttle, small alcohol fires burning in sand buckets throughout the room, trying to take the edge off of the radiant cold of the metal shuttle.

During the spring months the meeting was monthly and focused on elections and land allocations.

This meeting had been called, and as soon as the floor was opened, people started to worry about the Marines.

"They're spying on us!" a man shouted and Alec saw Bill Barnes, leaning on his daughter in the crowd.

"They are trying to keep us alive, you stubborn old jackass," Jessup shouted right back. "You should have told someone you were out of wood."

"You could have refused their help," Alec added and Jessup shot him an annoyed look. "Or you could have come into one of the shelters. You want to stay in your house and burn furniture, that's your choice, but don't complain when I send a runner out to check on you. And don't bitch that I asked a Marine to run for me. I am grateful for their help," Alec finished.

"You don't have a wife to get cuckolded, or a daughter to be seduced. Kid. What are you going to do when your girl gets raped by one of them?" Barnes shouted back at Alec and he identified the fear in the other man.

Jessup put his hand to his shoulder and Alec leaned forward to ignore it.

"I would be glad that my woman could still have a child when I am sterile," Alec said loudly. "Most of the third generation men are sterile, you know," he added.

"You think they're doing us a favor?" Barnes said and his daughter tried to calm him without success. "If you punks can't get a girl pregnant, why don't you just leave it to the men who come from Earth? We ain't shooting blanks."

Alec saw faces in the crowd shift from agreeing with the man to turning to see if he was thinking about what he was saying.

"People born on Earth have purer blood; we should be making a sperm bank from immigrants not some freak-show soldiers," Barnes finished and Alec watched his daughter straighten her shoulders and stare straight ahead.

"You start at home?" Westover challenged from the other side of Jessup.

The crowd was completely silent as people stared at Barnes and his pregnant daughter.

"My daughter was raped by one of those freaks!" Barnes shouted and pointed to Phillips and Lonco standing to the side of the chief's raised table platform.

"It wasn't rape," Westover said bluntly and pushed back from the table. "Earth-born have no immunity to the rot, thirty percent die quickly, and the rest only last a decade. Second generation without our DNA have a basic resistance and reach full human maturity but are mostly sterile, with our DNA the third generation is surviving," Westover explained patiently with his arms crossed in front of his body and a frown.

"I don't believe you!" Barnes shouted to interrupt him.

"Neither did Jacob Waits," Jessup said.

"Waits was a useless ass who bought his friends," Barnes replied, and Alec continued to watch the crowd to see who nodded to the man's comments.

"You campaigned for him," Jessup said with a smile. "Next ship of immigrants will have a new ass you can elect."

"I'll be dead by then," Barnes said and Alec watched the man shrink into himself. "Why do they have to rape our women?" he asked in a flat voice.

"It's never rape," Westover replied.

"You're calling good women a bad thing," Wayne Tranger said from the side of the room.

"Most women use the sperm bank without telling their families," Westover said without looking toward the deputy sheriff. "Others are recently widowed and open to a few nights of companionship. Sometimes a woman comes to me and asks for help, and asks for secrecy; and rarely, there is an affair. It's not rape."

"This is women's business and not a subject for men to debate as if we have a say," Jessup said firmly to the crowd.

"If the kid has my name and eats my food I can ask questions," another voice called out and Alec couldn't spot the source. "Jeff Wimmer said that the Marines are culling the third generation of bad DNA."

"Jeff didn't understand," Westover said.

"Understand what? My son died!" the man threw back.

"Frenz was a spirit. He thought he was helping the colony by killing the genetic dead-ends," Westover said slowly, and Alec saw Phillips move from the sideline to the front of the platform.

"My daughter is dead!" Ell Menedez shouted, her face red and worn.

"She was third-generation and had the early rot," Jessup said in a respectful voice and forced himself to return her tear-filled gaze.

"Eighteen children died that night," Phillips said, and Alec watched people still as they listened to the man's low voice. "Frenz had a list of twenty-eight third-generation children who are dying of the rot and he had the Cosery's name with a question mark because they are both healthy. The question mark is because a lot of the third generation are active empaths. Something I would strongly counsel that you not tell Earth," Phillips said and Alec wondered if anyone else saw Westover's lips move with his words.

"Five Marines got twenty-eight women pregnant?" Ell Menedez asked and looked from Phillips over to Lonco and back.

"Yes, ma'am," Lonco answered from the side.

"Just so they could die," Ell said in a defeated voice.

"Not all third generation, just the ones with bad genetics. About twenty percent," Phillips finished.

"What, the doctor doesn't get a slice of the pie?' Alec quipped, without thinking and half of the room chuckled.

"That would be a breach of my Hippocratic oath," Westover said. He didn't mention the sperm bank or the fact that he, Weistler, and the Colonel needed to be selective in choosing women due to racial genetics.

"So, we're all going to go crazy and suicide?" Kim asked from the front of the crowd.

"No, ma'am," Phillips responded.

"But, that's what the Marines did because of the telepathy and you said we're empaths," Kim said.

Alec leaned forward a bit more, his elbows on the table in front of him, watching the crowd.

"That was the hot-link, not the genetics. The empathy is coming from the planet. Not us," Phillips turned to walk toward the tarp door that covered the blasted airlock.

"Ask your elders," Westover added, and picked up his pile of papers from the table and followed the two Marines while the room silently waited.

"I am an elder," a swirl of soot and stove exhaust said from in front of the table.

Alec stood slightly to lean forward and look down on the spirit as others in the crowd pulled away.

"You are a good elder," Sheila agreed, and Alec watched her light a sage bundle from a stove and walk the smoke toward the spirit.

Seconds passed and the spirit moved the smoke to become a faint outline of Jacob Waits.

"I have a problem to put before our chief," Waits said in a formal voice.

"Where does the empathy come from?" Tammy Toms asked.

"The Chair recognizes the spirit of former Assistant Chief Jacob Waits," Jessup said in an equally formal voice.

"The cemetery needs to be moved into this shell to protect us from the weather. I do not want to crumble to gravel and pave someone's walkway," Waits said.

"The Marine said to ask our elders. Where does the empathy come from?" Kim said again, stepping toward Waits' spirit.

"The request to move the cemetery inhabitants into the shuttle cargo bay has been noted and will be addressed and voted at the next meeting," Jessup said.

"Damn it!" Kim shouted as Waits spirit swirled and started to break up.

"Nature finds a way," echoed through the room and Waits was gone.

"We're evolving," Ell Menedez said.

And Alec saw Sheila put her hand against her stomach.

#

"You looked like Westover's puppet," Jessup said and offered Phillips a beer.

He was sitting on the roof of the Admin building with a bucket fire at his feet, watching the dancing and laughter in the field below. Several hours had passed since the Marines left the council meeting. Jessup was just plain tired and wished Alec was ten years older, so he could step down and spend a few years fishing.

Phillips accepted the beer without comment and took the empty seat uninvited.

"When you talk, Westover's lips move," Jessup added.

"And when Westover talks, Weistler's lips move," Phillips said after drinking the beer dry and setting the bottle down beside himself.

"Why'd you walk away?" Jessup asked and thought that Phillips might have been interested in Waits comments about the stone bodies becoming gravel.

"It's too hard to run five bodies and interact with the Doc in a crowd of people," Phillips answered, and Jessup offered him a second beer. "When Toms died, we decided to move into the woods; we made a path. There's another clearing twenty miles to the North."

Jessup drank his beer without comment, not wanting to distract.

"We can't maintain this level of division in interaction much longer, people need to quit talking to us and let us work," Phillips said.

"Are you Westover's puppets?" Jessup asked, reached past the beers, and picked up a jug of raw whiskey strong enough to fuel the stove. He carefully poured some into the bucket of burning gravel in front of him.

"No," Phillips said and took the jug from him to drink several long swallows of the crude alcohol. "We melded in the link, but the Doc is mostly separate."

"Melded?" Jessup asked.

"Became one mind with five bodies, a skinwalker," Phillips said and took a third swallow of the whiskey.

"Alcohol help?" Jessup asked.

"Used to," Phillips said, setting the jug between them. "Some of the third generation help, they quiet the noise, make it easier to focus, you become a little separate from the link when they touch you."

"Because you changed our DNA?" Jessup prodded as the man leaned back in the chair and stretched his legs in front of him.

"The empaths are from the rot and the trees," Phillips said and took a single deep breath to start snoring.

Jessup picked up the jug and took a swallow, felt it burn straight through and leave him feeling warm and tired. He leaned back, his legs stretched to the side of the fuel burning bucket stove and let himself doze off to the beat of the drummers singing a grass song.

Chapter 19

Projected Earth date: 2132

Planet Date: 0105, Winter

Coyote's Winter House, Rex Tyrol, Designated Choctaw Emigration planet, Kanto Corporation

Three months later

"Smoke," Toni said and pointed across the valley toward the edge of the forest, in the direction of the Barnes farm.

Alec watched a thin puff of white smoke trail into the clear sky.

"Hey, Doc," Loko shouted down from the admin roof. "Hey, Doc," his twin echoed, shouting toward the medical clinic's slightly open door.

Alec balled up some wet snow and threw it at the clinic window just as Westover stepped outside and looked up. Winter was close to over, with the snow a soggy mess, ready to melt when the spring storm came.

The snowball was in flight, the man made eye contact, and as the snowball hit the window with more of a thud than a splat, Alec found himself staring down the barrel of a handgun.

"What the fuck do you want?" Westover shouted and Alec was relieved to see him holster the weapon.

"Smoke," Toni shouted down and pointed toward the growing column of gray smoke.

Westover walked over to climb the ladder, and Alec moved out of his way.

"House fire," Westover said after a quick glance.

"Is there anyone nearby?" Alec asked.

"How should I know?" Westover replied, and climbed back down the ladder.

"Are there any Marines near the fire?" Alec forced himself to say in a neutral tone. The doctor was irritable and still holding a grudge. Alec swung a leg over the edge of the roof and started down the ladder.

Westover stood, staring blankly with his lips moving, a few feet from the ladder and Alec walked past him to ring the alarm.

"Jackass," Westover said as the siren spun down and people came out of nearby buildings.

"What's up?" Jessup asked.

"House fire at about the Barnes place," Alec answered.

"Could be their barn," Wayne Tranger said.

"House," Westover said. "Lonco and Metzger are helping the daughter, father is dead of the rot and knocked over a lamp," he added.

"Shit," Wayne said. "Any chance of saving the house?"

"It's already gone," Westover said. His eyes closed. "Family will stay in the barn, refusing to come into town. I'm heading over."

"Who's hurt?" Alec asked.

"No one," Westover said and moved into his clinic.

"They'll need food and blankets right away," Wayne said.

"They're fine," Westover said. "They stocked the barn in case someone got trapped by the bugs."

"Smart," Jessup said and Alec nodded.

"We should set up little corner stations with everything to survive, one room, stove, made of solid stone," Alec said. "Put them at every intersection and on the corners of fields."

"Good idea," Wayne said.

"Hey, Doc, mind if I walk out with you?" Alec asked as Westover started across the open courtyard, passed the red pole, and turned onto the path that would eventually lead to the edge of the forest.

"Suit yourself," Westover replied without waiting.

#

"Saying I would rather cart things out that they don't need than walk out there and have to come back for shit," Wayne said.

Sheila paused in the doorway to the admin building. It was above freezing and the wind was calm, as she hesitated on the threshold.

"Hey, Sheila," Beth said.

"Hey, Sheriff," Sheila replied and moved inside, closing the door behind her. "I brought a blanket and some food for the Barnes," she said and placed her bag into an open box on top of the already loaded cart.

"We're waiting for a Marine to confirm what they need before making the trip," Beth said with a glare toward her deputy.

"The Marines do not know we are waiting for a message," Wayne said bluntly.

"Trey left my house after the siren, he said that there was beans and rice and fuel for the lanterns but not enough wood for heat," Sheila offered, not wanting to get in the argument that she suspected she had interrupted. "I put salt, savory, and thyme in my bag with butter and dried carrots. And a jar of sweet lime. I wish I had more to spare."

"That's very generous of you," Beth said.

"It's going to be dark soon," Wayne said. "It sounds like they can survive the night. I'll head out at first dawn."

"Wait for me," Jessup said as Sheila opened the door to leave. "The Marines, the doctor, and our deputy chief will be out there tonight, it's the rest of the town I worry about," Jessup joked as he came around the cart to join her at the door.

Sheila watched Beth and Wayne nod at the comment.

"We'll both take a walk about, Chief," Beth said.

"I'll cover here to Sheila's and back to my house," Jessup said and Sheila moved out into the cold.

The temperature had fallen since she went inside and the clear sky told her that the spring storm was at least one more day away.

"You don't have to walk me home," she said as Jessup walked silently beside her.

"This route saves Beth and Wayne a couple of hours,'" Jessup said, and Sheila knew it wasn't the complete truth.

"You could just tell me what it is you want to say and take the fork straight home," Sheila said with a nod to the split in the road ahead.

The path looped wide, away from her house to go through a cluster of other houses before coming back closer to the town center and directly in front of her door.

They made their way past Patty's empty house and she thought about asking someone to help her move Nillie's statue from the garden and into her living room after the melt. Behind Patty's house the field was a maze of snow forts and piled sled hills that were abandoned and treacherous in the late winter as everyone waited for the rains. They walked in silence until Sheila's small house came into view.

"You called him Trey," Jessup said, staring at Patty's dark windows.

"That's his name," Sheila said, watching him.

"Was. That was his name," Jessup said and for a moment Sheila felt her world fall.

Her knees went weak and her heart pounded as the panic flooded her with the memory of losing Ryan; but a calm spot in the center of her body refused to accept what he said and she held the calmness in her mind until the panic was gone.

"Was?" she asked Jessup.

"They melded together in that hot-link," Jessup said, and refused to meet her gaze.

"I know," Sheila replied quietly, thinking about the moments when she couldn't tell who was in the house before looking to see which Marine stopped by to check on her.

"Phillips said there was only one mind in the five bodies," Jessup continued and Sheila watched his breath billow out as the sun fell below the tree line and the temperature dropped further.

"You said Phillips."

"He said that third-generation are empaths and touching one gives a little bit of separation," Jessup said and finally turned in the dim light to face her.

"So, one-and-a-fifth minds in five bodies?" Sheila joked without feeling.

"Something like that," Jessup agreed.

"I wonder, if each Marine carried around a third gen kid on his back, how long it would take to be five minds?" Sheila asked and then smiled at the image of the men with a papoose sling on their backs.

"That's a thought," Jessup agreed and chuckled out loud. "Have a nice night," he added as he walked away.

Sheila stood for several minutes in the dark and Metzger opened her front door. She followed him inside the house without saying anything.

#

"You lied," Westover said, staring at the kid.

Let it go.

He lied, Westover thought. *He's not sterile.*

Whatever gets you laid.

"About what?" the assistant chief asked as he set down the arm full of wood he carried into the barn.

The sun was down and the moonlight shining in through the single high window, cast deep shadows in the open barn. Westover moved back toward the huddle of civilians by the single fire without answering.

"About what?" he heard behind him again, and he smiled at the teen's annoyance.

Are you deliberately baiting him?

He might not know.

He's never asked to be tested, Westover countered.

"Thank you," Westover said and accepted a spot by the fire next to Nina Barnes.

She going to pop a maggot soon?

No.

"About what?" Alec demanded of Trey.

Westover gritted his teeth in frustration.

He's an ambitious, self-serving jackass, Westover thought and pushed himself out of the link.

He's your kid, pushed back just as hard and Westover dropped his cup of lukewarm coffee without being aware of his body. The visual memory of his own genetic records flooded his sight and he blinked against the truth that he had been blocking.

"Fuck!" Westover said.

"It's my fault, Doctor, I'll get you a new cup," Nina said and struggled to stand as Westover processed his own reaction.

He looks like you.

"About what?"

"You never got tested for sterile," Trey mouthed.

"I used the school microscope," Alec answered and Westover had a hard time seeing the new cup of stale coffee offered him for listening to the conversation as Trey and the boy moved toward the back of the barn to round up the five loose cows and get them into empty stalls.

Every man born on this rock is sterile until between sixteen and twenty-three. The fungus interferes with testosterone expression. Delays puberty and maturity. Westover pretended to sip as he fed information into the link.

"Your testicles drop and get hard?" Trey asked.

What? Westover asked with a forced civility.

"Yeah," the kid responded.

"You might not be sterile," Trey said. "The rot slows down puberty, takes longer to grow a pair."

You're joking. You're fucking joking.

"Oh," The kid said as they pushed the first cow into a stall and closed the door. "I wish the Doc had explained that in class. The guys all figure we're sterile."

Westover took a swallow of the coffee and mentally watched as Trey opened the second stall and Alec walked the next cow in. A blur at the corner of his mind pulled at his attention and he gave the stall a cursory scan for life, looking for puppies or rats, only to have his mind pulled into a black hole of screaming and pain.

No! He tried to shout against the echo of hell as his body stopped and he felt his connection to the link be replaced by thousands of moving, twisting thoughts that never quite formed. The force of the screaming panic of thoughts shifted and filled with a warm presence as their attention moved from tearing at his mind to fighting to get to the warmth. Trying to find a spot to claim before the cold returned.

Westover felt himself mentally yanked out of the hive by the trees as Trey physically drug the boy back from the edge of a sinkhole that had swallowed the second cow.

Report! Echoed through him, and Westover sat up to survey his body and then stood to jog across the barn floor to Trey and Alec.

Bugs, Westover thought and saw Trey's surprise as his arm rested on Alec's. The kid offered the same buffer to the link as Sheila even though he was only second generation.

The barn is on rock!

Not enough rock, Westover replied and gave Trey a look that included his hand on the boy's arm, and Trey stepped sideways to rejoin the link.

Talk to the daughter about construction.

"We need to kill the cow and grubs," Westover said out loud, with a glance at Nina Barnes.

Trey walked carefully to the edge of the hole and looked down.

Six feet below, the cow lay on the ground beneath the barn, and Westover could see hundreds of bugs that crawled onto it to lay eggs when the floor boards gave way in a clean circle where they were chewed.

"I need some fire," Trey said as the body of the cow deformed from the grubs within.

Nina Barnes walked into the stall and handed him her lantern. He hesitated until she was gone, and then dropped it into the hole beside the cow.

Westover stood beside Alec, looking through Trey's eyes and heard the rustle of bug wings as they stirred from their cluster.

Westover watched the ground that the cow was on shift and ripple as the bugs absorbed the lantern into their mass and then spit it and dozens of dead bugs back out.

The lantern broke and the fuel spread the flames and the bugs started to burn as Trey continued to lean over the hole and watch.

Get back before they swarm!

Westover saw it. In the light of the fire that was building on the surface of the swarm, he saw the slick of the rot at the edges and the small stones falling free as the mass tried to move clear of the fire.

Get out!

"Get everybody out," Westover said to Alec and trusted the boy as he moved forward to grab Trey's arm and pull him back from the edge of the pit.

Quit being Weistler and get your ass outside, Marine! Westover shouted into the link with Phillips' voice, and felt a bitter pain in response.

Fuck you!

But he moved and Westover followed as the sound of bug wings chased them from the barn and into the freezing night.

#

Sheila rose alone with the first dawn. She hadn't slept and the light gave her an excuse to get up and start breakfast. She enjoyed cooking for the men. They came and left on a schedule she hadn't figured out, and Jessup's words kept echoing through her head as she moved into her kitchen and put a pot of water on to boil for coffee.

She knelt to add wood to the fire and heard someone behind her. It was Trey's footsteps, and as she stood, she was disappointed to see Weistler with an armload of firewood.

She moved out of his way silently and started to mix up a bowl of pancake batter.

"Bacon?" he asked.

"Yes, please," Sheila said and watched him walk to the kitchen door and exit to retrieve the meat from the hang shed under her eave.

Minutes later, the first cups of coffee were poured and she put the bacon into her oven as he added the exact amount of cream she liked without being told and stirred her coffee for her.

"Thank you," she said and wondered if he could feel her tension.

He turned away from her and moved to the pantry to retrieve the jar of sweet lime syrup Trey dripped onto his pancakes.

She didn't look up when he brought it and set it on the counter. She turned and stared out the window at the dusty snow and the wisp of smoke from her neighbor's chimney.

He moved to wash the previous night's dishes and Sheila turned back toward him to watch his profile. Weistler was shorter and darker-skinned and his gray hair was high on his forehead with a widow's peak.

Then he pursed his lips in the exact same frown as Trey as he sloshed the dishes in the bowl to rinse off the soap. She stepped toward him as he turned away to put the dishes on the far counter, and she reached up to scratch lightly at his back.

He stopped moving, dropped his arms to his side, and she scratched her nails in a circular motion over one shoulder and then the next. It was something she did for Trey and he always responded with a sigh before turning to kiss her, and Sheila continued to scratch for several long minutes until he sighed and then turned and her upraised hand traveled from his back shoulder to his chest.

He leaned forward and for a moment Sheila wanted to let him kiss her, but she ducked her head at the last minute and his lips pressed against her forehead, and she stood frozen with her hand on his chest waiting for him to pull away.

He raised his hand to reach behind her and held her lightly, his lips on her forehead, and she didn't move.

Minutes passed and the kitchen door opened and Sheila felt cold when Weistler released her and walked to the front of the house, leaving her in the kitchen with Trey. She moved to take the boiling water from the heat, pulled the almost-burnt bacon from the stove, and started to wash more dishes when Trey stopped her with his hand on her shoulder and she turned toward him.

He looked into her eyes and then moved forward to kiss her lips softly.

#

"The bugs get the rot?" Wayne asked and Alec looked around the crowd.

Westover sat beside Chief Jessup while Alec leaned against the wall by the side door. The town meeting was inside a barn; the shuttle cargo bay slowly filled with family statues that were carried from gardens and yards and occasionally houses. Jacob Waits' spirit visited dozens of people, always focused on asking for the remains of the dead to be protected, always saying that he didn't want to decay into gravel and come to an end.

Alec tried to talk to the dead man when he materialized the morning after Barnes' barn burned. Waits repeated that the weather destroys the minds of the elders, and Alec asked what about the minds of the bugs. Waits' spirit had swirled and started to spin apart as the man stared in fear over his shoulder at an empty doorway and then he said, "Plow the fields," and dissolved.

"Everything on this planet gets the rot," Westover said. "The flutterbys get the rot. Young hunter trees get the rot. Hell, the chief tells me even big Moogies get the rot."

And people stared at the doctor.

"Silver grass doesn't get the rot," Wayne said, and Alec saw several people nod.

"Silver grass is just a plant," Westover said impatiently.

"And the hunter tree isn't?" Wayne shot back.

"I don't know what the hunter trees are," Westover admitted. "The surveys were done in the winter season and I can find no record of them even being scanned."

"May I have the floor?" Alec asked and stepped forward. Beth had been drilling him on protocol and he found the forced politeness fun to play.

Westover waived his hand impatiently and Jessup nodded.

"The hunter trees talk. I've heard them, the Marines have heard them, and most of the third generation can hear them. They're awake," Alec said and only the immigrants looked disbelieving as others nodded. "If you don't believe they talk, go take a walk by the forest wall without a couple blasts in your pocket," he challenged a man who gave an angry glare.

"The hunter trees are intelligent. The flutterbys play with children and puppies, teasing them and playing catch-me, yet they change course if the kid or dog is headed for saw grass, they will shit on the path in front of you if you're in a bad mood, and sometimes they drop down and sit beside people who are crying or sad. I think flutterbys are emotionally aware of us and that makes them at least as smart as dogs. Patty and Ryan's dog Nillie is now a spirit."

Alec looked around the room and saw people thinking about his words.

"And I know the goddamned moogies are smart and aware. Just get one wrapped around your face while fishing and you can hear the damn thing laugh. Moogies don't care about death and I've only ever heard their emotions as jackasses laughing at their own joke," Alec said and paused to consider his next words.

"They're mean," Toni called from the back of the room. "The emotions are pleasure from your pain. The more afraid you are the more they laugh, right up until you cook them and then they're just annoyed as they die."

Alec nodded and saw most of the younger fishermen nod as well.

"The trees aren't really trees," he said. "The hunter trees are closer to a giant equisetum. A horsetail on earth," Alec said. "It's a giant hollow plant that pulls minerals from the rocks and spreads by spores not seeds."

"The giant trees are hollow?" Jessup asked.

"Yes," Alec confirmed. "I pulled photos from the first and second colony and found they blasted dozens of them out of our clearing. There was always a hollow center, just like on the sprouts."

"So, the sprouts aren't coming off of roots?" Peter asked.

"No, spores."

"Like the rot," Wayne asked.

"Wait," Westover interjected. "Back up one point?"

"Sure," Alec said with eye contact to acknowledge Wayne.

"Horsetail?" Westover asked.

"Yeah, really similar," Alec confirmed.

"Pulling minerals up into the plant?"

"Yeah, it's in the second colony's initial survey notes," Alec said.

"I never saw those notes in the files," Westover challenged.

"Paper notes," Alec offered, "in the admin files."

"It should be in the medical files," Westover threw back.

"Problem, Doctor?" Jessup asked.

"Horsetail concentrates silica," Westover replied. "The rot deposits silica in the body until it blooms. The goddamn tea is feeding the rot."

And the room was dead silent as Alec looked from the angry Doctor to Jessup and back.

"Are you sure?" Kim asked.

"The rot deposits silica throughout the body. That's the arthritis. When you get too much silica the rot blooms and you're dead," Westover said in a slow, forced voice.

"No one connected tea drinking to early rot?" Wayne pushed.

"Why would they?" Westover replied. "Fucking guinea pigs."

"The trees are like horsetails," Alec restated when no one spoke. "We should talk about the tea next month."

"Yes," Jessup said in a subdued voice. "Spores are like pollen, maybe the white pollen clouds that come the second week after the spring rains?" he changed the subject and people nodded.

"The trees are smart, the flutterbys have emotions, and the moogies are crazy," Alec said slowly, re-schooling his thoughts. "That leaves the bugs. The Marines saw rot on the edges of the swarm in the Barnes' barn."

"I saw it, too," Nina Barnes called out.

"The barn was built in the middle of a flat bedrock outcropping. It had a hole six-feet-wide by twenty-feet-deep from where a hunter tree had been. The tree made the hole," Alec said, and finally glanced down at his notes.

"Makes sense," Westover said. "A two-foot-tall horsetail can have a ten-foot taproot, and they have been known to erode rock on Earth by depositing gravel and then grinding with the sway of the plant in the wind."

Alec made eye contact with Westover and nodded. The man's attitude toward him had not softened so much as now he treated Alec with the respect Alec had only seen him give the Marines.

"There are ten to fifteen more of those holes under houses somewhere in this valley," Alec said.

"With bugs?" Jessup asked.

"I think so," Alec said. "The bugs get the rot. The spirits talk about angry, hungry minds circling the fire. I think that's the bugs."

"You think they're intelligent?" Wayne asked.

"They are," Westover answered. "We've had telepathic contact with them and the trees."

"But not the moogies or the flutterbys?" Nina asked.

"We eat moogies and flutterbys," Phillips responded.

"We need to stop," Alec said. "Eating the flutterbys, anyway. Ross said there was a tree, a flutterby, and an elder by the fire. The Cosery grandmother said there were lost minds circling the fire with the bugs."

"She didn't say they were bugs," Phillips corrected.

"I think the flutterbys are self-aware and we shouldn't eat them," Alec said and several people in the room nodded.

"Back to the point," Jessup said. "Do we have a map of the rock holes?"

"No," Alec admitted. "The Barnes' barn was noted because it was against the ridgeline. There was one next to the second colony power plant that they used as a cold storage."

"We had one under our house," Jeff Wimmer said. "My brother's house," he added.

"I think there's going to be a spring hatch," Alec said.

"Did you find a record of a spring hatch in the files?" Wayne asked.

"No," Alec said.

"It makes sense," Westover agreed. "The bugs in Barnes's barn were in a hibernation cluster. That means they've overwintered before."

"Shit," Wayne said.

"Yeah," Alec agreed. "I think there will be a spring hatch and I think the bugs have spirits that push them and guide their evolution."

"Fuck," Jessup said.

"I'd like to try something," Alec said after several minutes of silence.

"Do not try to talk to a bug," Westover said bluntly and several people laughed at the impatience in his voice.

"Don't talk to the trees, they answer," Phillips added.

"Doctor Westover said that he called one of the dead Marines into a spirit by concentrating on him," Alec explained.

"Fuck that!" Sheila exclaimed from beside Phillips.

"Dr. Bill Kim was an immigrant in the second colony. He was an," and Alec glanced down to study his single page of notes. "A bug scientist, says in a record that he was studying our bugs. I can't find any actual notes on the bugs in the files."

"Kanto Corp or the UN kept the notes," Phillips said.

"I want us to concentrate on him and see if we can pull him into a spirit so we can ask him questions," Alec said and looked from Jessup to Westover for approval.

Westover nodded first.

"Do you have a picture of him?" Phillips asked.

"No," Alec admitted. "He was Korean and Choctaw. He painted and he played a flute and he came after his wife's death and brought his daughter, Elle Kim."

With that, a swirl of air stirred the straw on the floor between Alec and Jessup.

"Water," Sheila said, and Phillips moved forward to pour Westover's undrunk coffee onto a bucket stove.

"He studied in Boston and paid for a piano to be shipped here,"

"For Elle to practice," a voice whispered and the spirit of a small man took form.

"We need your help," Alec said, and the dust started to fall from the spirit.

"Your daughter was beautiful," Phillips said, and Alec watched the spirit gain form.

"She sang like a bird," the spirit said.

"Is she with you?" Phillips asked.

"She stays by the fire; there are no birds on this world," the old man's ghost responded.

"Is the fire a good place to be?" Phillips prodded.

"Yes, it is comfortable and easy to sleep by," the spirit responded and drifted slowly closer to Phillips.

"I'm glad your daughter is safe now," Phillips said.

"Uncle?" Alec spoke when the spirit didn't.

"The native Symphyta-like creature that wants to be of the order of Hymenoptera?" the spirit asked and turned toward Alec.

"The bugs," Alec said.

And the spirit sighed.

"Can they hatch in spring?" Alec asked.

"Child," the spirit said patiently. "They live five years, they sleep in the winter, they swarm when a hive is disturbed."

"But," Alec looked from the spirit to Westover and back. "The worms come out of the forest." And the spirit drifted toward the fire bucket as Phillips poured a bit more coffee onto the flame. "The bugs come from the worms and burrow, then come back out of the ground to lay eggs and the grubs eat people."

"The saw fly that burrows into the ground lives five years drinking sap from the hunter trees before rising and laying eggs on a flutterby or a cow or a human. We gave them so many menu options," he explained with a new sigh.

"The swarm cycle is twenty-seven years," Westover said after a glance to Phillips.

"They lied," Phillips said.

"What triggers the swarm? Was it the storm?" Alec asked.

"They swarm when they overpopulate. When they saturate the tree roots. When the ground gets too wet. When they fight a new swarm trying to invade," the spirit whispered as it started to dissolve. "They want to be Hymenoptera."

"Uncle!" Alec shouted. "How do we-" and the spirit was gone.

"They lied," Jessup agreed. "Spring hatch people, we need to get underneath the older houses and look for hibernating swarms."

"What the hell is Hymenoptera?" Wayne asked.

Chapter 20

Projected Earth date: 2132

Planet Date: 0105, Spring

Coyote's Winter House, Rex Tyrol, Designated Choctaw Emigration planet, Kanto Corporation

Left! Martin Cosery repeated to himself as he ran along the path. *Left – ball hand. Left, ahead, away from the school, loop out, then back. The side of the path away from the siren. Don't go off the path. Run, turn left, keep running.*

The sky flashed white and he saw the dead flutterby in front of him. Saw the bug preparing to fly. And he jumped. Not high, not long. Just jumped as he ran and continued to run with yet another bug behind him.

The thunder was slow and building, and the air burned his nose and throat as he ran the long loop away from town center. *Gramma!* He tried to whisper as he ran, but he had no air and he needed to spit and his lungs burned.

His little brother, Tommy, and Jeff were hiding in the pantry. No one would help them. Martin pressed his right hand into his side against the pain and ran for the emergency siren.

#

Did you hear that?

Third generation.

No words.

Panic.

Fear.

Heading toward town.

Westover.

And Westover sat up, trying to hear the mind his men felt. A small echo in the link, an image of an old woman, and a faint impression of pain came to him.

That's the woman who stood down Frenz.

Spirit.

Martin Cosery.

And the siren spooled up outside of his office.

Shit.

The sound died back down just as a new lightening flash lit the valley and Westover looked outside in time to see the boy fall to the ground underneath the emergency siren's crank.

He threw the door open, scanned the sky and rooflines, watched the path in front of him and ran to the boy's side.

"Bugs!" Martin gasped as he struggled to breathe.

Waits' house.

Westover stood, put his back to the wall, and watched the boy for grubs while using his left hand to crank the siren for a solid minute.

It was almost midnight and the spring thaw was well underway, the temperature having risen to above freezing at night and the river ice was singing louder by the day. The rains would come in the morning, when the thunder and lightning passed.

Westover released the siren crank and picked up the boy, running across the open area to his office, and slammed the door behind him, setting the boy onto his own cot.

In the dim light, his vision flooded by Phillips running behind Weistler, his heart threatened to seize, and Westover concentrated to force Phillips to slow down.

Fuck off! Echoed through the link at his interference.

Tranger's house ahead, brief him! Westover threw back and didn't release control.

When Phillips and Weistler were inside the chief's house, Westover shifted his concentration and found Metzger and Lonco helping Tommy and Wimmer from the pantry, three dead bugs on the kitchen counter, and the sound of a swarm on the roof. Lonco looked over and watched a bug crawl through the cold kitchen stove pipe's flue vent and fall onto the counter.

"You're out of wood," Metzger said and hit the bug with a bat before reaching up to close the flue. Metallic scratching in the pipe echoed through the kitchen as Jeff Wimmer nodded his head.

"I was going to bring in wood in the morning," the frightened man said.

Clear? Westover asked.

Clear.

Trey? Westover probed the link and saw Sheila's face as the last Marine woke slowly.

"Shit!"

Westover saw Sheila pull back in surprise as his vision spun and Trey was pulling on his boots.

"Stay," Sheila said, and Trey looked back to her, the link flooding with her concern and regret.

"There are bugs at the Waits' house. Stay here," Trey answered. Westover watched her expression of resignation and not surprise.

"Be safe," she whispered as Trey cleared the bedroom doorway and ran for the front of the house.

Westover flooded the link with a quick situation report, including Phillips' heart attack, and watched as Trey exited the house cautiously.

Weistler and Jessup were running toward the Cosery neighborhood with pockets full of blasts, and Westover saw a dead dog on the path with grubs emerging as Phillips walked toward town. Phillips used a blast to kill the grubs, but gave the dog a wide berth on the trail before jogging away from the carcass toward the path intersection Trey was heading toward. He glanced down to see a single dim light on the side of his press-gun.

Trey had a red flashlight and ran, shifting the light in the night, trying to catch movement.

"Hey!" Alec shouted, and Trey paused to shine his light toward the young assistant chief and his mechanic girlfriend, running toward him on the right hand path.

He moved the flashlight up, to avoid blinding them, and the beam of light hit a bug as it circled above them.

Westover watched from Trey's eyes as he pushed forward, increasing his run speed with a last burst, and tackled Alec.

A searing pain lanced through the link and Westover isolated it to Trey's right shoulder just as a new lightning flash streaked across the sky and the hard crack of the bolt striking a hunter tree nearby drowned out the thunder. Westover yanked Trey's body and rolled the Marine onto his back, and felt the bug crunch under his weight.

He looked up and saw Phillips scanning the sky with his own light, looking for more bugs, and heard the girl gasp.

Westover blinked and he was looking down at Trey as the Marine rolled onto his side. His shoulder was already starting to distend.

He tried to buffer the link, tried to protect his men from the sensation of the grubs growing in the muscle wall. The scrape of mandibles on bone.

Westover started to order Alec to touch Trey, to mute the pain that flooded the link, but the whomph of a press-gun sounded and Westover saw both the barrel of Phillips' gun and Treys eyes as he died, and the link was silent for a moment.

Fuck!

Get moving!

Rain!

Rain? Westover demanded and Weistler pushed the sense of ice-cold drops hitting his face as he ran.

And then he forced the link and used Phillips to talk to Alec. "Phillips cannot run," he said and felt the angry push back. "Get inside for the night."

#

Westover opened his door when Phillips finally made it to the town center. Alec carried his shotgun like he had some training and the girl, Kim, helped Phillips walk as the pain in his chest faded to a dull, nauseating weight that made every step a trial just to push forward.

An echo of Phillips' original independence had tried to insist on being left in the dark, but Westover wasn't ready to lose another man and the others in the link were safe enough. Westover tried to grab his bag and run out to get a dose of homemade aspirin and some corn silk extract into him to slow the damage, but enough of Phillips remained in the link to override him and Westover was forced to monitor his patient from the safety of his office, while Martin Cosery made a pot of coffee and drank two cups before offering one.

The Marines confirmed bugs in a surprisingly narrow area around the neighborhood of the

Waits/Cosery house and the chief was sitting with a quiet Lonco on the back porch throwing blasts into the sinkhole that had opened beside the garden shed. Metzger and Weistler were jogging the trail on auto-pilot in an ever-widening loop around the valley as the rain fell. Just scanning for movement or sound.

Clear?

Clear, Westover answered when Phillips was inside and the door was closed.

"Alec, sit beside him and hold his hand," Westover said making eye contact with the kid.

Fuck you.

"I need to cut him from the link a bit so Metzger can take the focus," Westover explained.

"How does that work?" Kim demanded as she took Alec's shotgun and moved to stand beside the door.

Westover had his battered stethoscope and was trying to separate the rhythm as he used his free hand to hold out a glass of murky liquid to Phillips. The stethoscope had been on the planet when he landed. His own physiolink had died ten years ago and he nearly prayed as he dropped out of the link, closed his eyes, and concentrated on the sounds in his own ears. Using the patient's body to monitor and affect an emergency only provided so much information, and Westover

calmed his own beat until he could hear the slosh,
blubble, mur of Phillips' struggling heart.

The link pushed to reform and Westover took a
moment to scan. Lonco was still sitting beside the chief,
Metzger was focal, and Weistler trailed him in the dark
as they approached the community barns, a single
smudge fire ahead. Phillips was completely separate
from the link and Westover reached out telepathically
to find a clone of the hot-linked Marines and not the
man that once held the body. A separate and functional
copy of the merged men that resented the care and
attention Westover was giving.

"You aren't Phillips," Westover said in his best
conversational doctor voice as he moved across the
room and retrieved more aspirin.

"Neither was Trey," Phillips replied without
emotion.

"I had hoped," Westover said and let the
statement drop as Phillips drank the bitter tea solution
without care.

"So did we," Phillips said as he handed back the
empty cup and Westover added a bit more water,
rinsing the aspirin in a circle and drinking the dredge
himself.

The dry bitterness of the aspirin grain hit the
back of his throat and Westover struggled not to cough
for a minute.

The mention of Trey started him to thinking as he listened to Phillips heart once more and was satisfied that he had done what he could with the limited pharmacology available.

"Trey," Westover thought and said and focused on the dead Marine only to hear a faint echo and lose the focus.

Westover stood and moved across the room again to retrieve his cold, native coffee and take a drink, trying to clear the last of the bitter residue from his mouth.

Why Trey?

I wanted to ask about the fire.

It should have been Phillips' body. Trey had fifty more years.

And for the first time since they followed the widow back from the trees, Westover looked at Phillips. His hair was dirty and white, his face was a pale, faded black, and the wrinkles moved down his face until the skin hung from his chin. He was old, and Westover added twenty-six years to his landing age of fifty-three and wondered how many more years were spent in cryo from one planet to the next.

There was a limit to the human body's ability to endure the induced hibernation pods, and even Pro-gen didn't give you much of an edge. "Five years under, ten years out – ten years under, never again" was the standard. That and "Twenty-five will make you ninety." There was a hard, biological limit to how many years a person could use cryo and while one could tolerate twice as many years in short hops as in long trips, a career officer like Phillips would have maxed out his safety buffer and kept accepting missions.

Phillips looked decades older than his known seventy-eight years and Westover decided that he had to be past ninety and closer to one hundred.

One hundred and eight, echoed through the link with a chuckle.

Damn.

Allans.

What? Westover asked.

Allans is by the fire. Call him.

"*Allans,*" Westover said out loud as he focused into the link and concentrated on the Marine.

The echo of Trey touched him again and then the spirit was forming, his bleeding amputation still tightly bound at the wrist.

"Report," Westover said and the spirit faded until Martin Cosery poured water onto the hot burner above the bucket fire.

"Report what?" Allans asked after a glance at Westover that showed no recognition.

"I need a current Situation Report on the trees, the fire, and those that surround it," Westover barked in his best Phillips impersonation and pushed it through the link at the man.

Allans snapped to attention for a moment and then relaxed to move to stand beside Phillips and stare down at Alec's hand on Phillips' arm.

"The trees think of fire as rebirth, they have a mental fire to mark the spirit life. The flutterbys think of fire as lift, life, and safety, and join the trees when they wake after death. The colonists are American Indigenous and when they died and saw a fire that's where they went. One big happy camp of people just waiting for the next afterlife," Allans said and reached out his hand to touch Phillips' arm.

The mist and dust left a mark as the spirit lowered itself to stare into the eyes of the former Lieutenant Colonel Phillips' body.

"Let go," Allans whispered, and Alec looked to Westover who nodded and moved closer.

Jesus fucking Christ Almighty! Phillips said from outside his body and a new spirit formed beside Allans, looked down at his old body, and dissolved.

"Let the body die," Allans said as he moved away from Phillips and started to dissolve.

"Explain!" Westover barked.

"It's a soul trap, the fungus, an organic computer that circles the planet in a fog. So many random memories and pieces of minds just waiting to focus and form. Those that make it to the fire can search out the lost pieces of themselves. Most never see the fire. Most never notice they died. I didn't know until you told me, didn't notice the time or know that I was dead. Now I sit by the fire and trade memories like food and wish to hell you had not told me," Allans finished with a sigh.

"The bugs?" Westover probed.

"The bugs are like suicides and the insane. They run through the fog screaming and can't let go of the pain."

"Phillips didn't die of the rot," Alec said, and Westover glanced at the kid to see a man who looked just like he remembered seeing himself, the day he was stranded on the planet.

"Patterns are patterns, it's all in the fungus. The Colonel died before the first snowfall when his mind merged with the link. You all die one by one and are still here," Allans said and his spirit simply quit holding the dust and moisture together.

"Everyone gets the rot," Alec said.

"So everyone becomes a spirit," Westover agreed.

Not everyone finds the fire, his men said, and Westover felt the echo of Phillips.

\#

Sheila sat in the kitchen, feeding the fire and trying not to think.

"Jacob RunsLightly," her mother whispered.

"Why Ryan?" Sheila replied.

"I froze," a man echoed behind her.

Sheila looked up from the fire, blinking against the bright spots in her vision and tried to see her first husband.

"I love you and I was afraid and I froze," Ryan said from in front of her.

"I love you," Sheila whispered as she felt the tears begin to build.

"You'll lose him, too," Ryan said and moved closer to her.

"Trey?" Sheila asked and felt his absence in her heart. The feeling of being watched had finally left her minutes after Trey ran into the night and she knew he was dead.

"The skinwalker lives," Ryan said with a hint of impatience and Sheila almost felt guilty for asking her dead husband about her lover. "Jacob RunsLightly will become and breathe and then walk to the fire so we can see our way home. You will lose him, too."

And the kitchen was empty.

Sheila sat, listening to the rain until first dawn gave way to true morning sunshine and the fire was dead.

She heard the kitchen door open behind her and the man moved to stand beside the sink and used a towel to dry his hair of the rain. He went back outside and brought in an armload of firewood and she felt a scream build inside of her, fighting against the silence.

And then, for a moment, she felt watched. Only a moment and the man behind her stepped around her to turn and face her and she saw Metzger. Rain-soaked and exhausted. He offered her the towel to wipe the dried tears from her face and she stood as she accepted the offer, using the rain's dampness to rub her eyes.

"He's dead," Sheila said.

"We all are," Metzger responded.

"I don't want to be alone," Sheila whispered.

"You will never be alone," Metzger said and stepped forward to cup her face and bring her lips to his in a soft kiss that broke her heart as the feeling of being watched came back to her.

:

Thank you for reading.

I have a web comic:

http://zombpocalypse.cartoonistsleague.org/

https://www.facebook.com/TalesfromtheZombi
eApocalypse

And you can find me on Facebook at:

https://www.facebook.com/cheryceclayton

The artist can be contacted at:

https://www.facebook.com/pages/JinxMedic-
Studios/154366657980647

I will be releasing new stories monthly, watch my Facebook for events, free stories, contests, and random rants.

Please leave a review.